# JJC

DUMO KAIZER J ORUOBU

authorHOUSE®

*AuthorHouse™ UK*
*1663 Liberty Drive*
*Bloomington, IN 47403  USA*
*www.authorhouse.co.uk*
*Phone: 0800.197.4150*

*Published by AuthorHouse  12/29/2017*

*ISBN: 978-1-5462-8611-0 (sc)*
*ISBN: 978-1-5462-8610-3 (e)*

*Print information available on the last page.*

*Any people depicted in stock imagery provided by Thinkstock are models,*
*and such images are being used for illustrative purposes only.*
*Certain stock imagery © Thinkstock.*

*This book is printed on acid-free paper.*

# CONTENTS

## TELEPHONE CONTACTS AND EMAIL ADDRESSES:

+23484666622 + 234 7042220012, +234 8073333123,
+234 0899881004, +234 8171234557, +234 8133444423,
+234 8053532222, +234 9087123456, +234 9081112345,
+234 8091124477, +234 9099770100, +234 9080000978,
+234 8055556633, +234 8091234249, +234 7032476611,
+234 8079787214, +234 8098412345, +234 8033201557,
+234 8039606306, +234 9085123456, +234 9086123456,
+234 8189111555, +234 9091234344, +234 8089358559,
+234 8168956384, +234 9085312345, +234 9085412345,
+234 8072220006, +234 9099133311, +234 9099133335,
+234 9099133337, +234 9087812345, +234 8168956384,
+234 9099771332, +234 8171234523, +234 8060069993.

Email: doruobu@gmail.com, doruobu@yahoo.com, kingfisherafrique@yahoo.com

# PUBLICATIONS

Dumo Oruobu has to his credit twenty seven Music Albums in The Highlife Tradition on the market and the publication of nine Books between June 30 and November 30, 2016, including –

1. Wife For Sale?
2. Silence Of Breaking Day
3. Tears Of The Guilty
4. Keinba
5. Loveache
6. Phones At War
7. Invisible Tears
8. The Eleven Brothers Of Joseph
9. The Penguin And His Love

# QUOTATION MARKS AS OFFENSIVE REFEREES' WHISTLE

My experimentation with doing away completely with Quotation Marks has been sustained here in JJC for the same reasons that I have given in all other cases in my foray into the wide Ocean of living in the World of make believe of Fiction – that when we speak to ourselves in our everyday interactions, we understand each other even with the reality which we know and face that those little inverted comas are not graphically painted and pasted there in front of us as we speak on every known subject, theme and style – as we even act out whole full length dramas.

Those marks, I believe, interrupt the flow of what we read as they make us pause now and again to reflect on what they are supposed to signpost to us.

Our reading is more racy and more pleasurable without the Quotation Marks than with them looming large in front of us, while their absence makes us stay focused in the actions that we are following, in exactly the same way as we feel when the Referee's whistle is silent during the run of beautiful soccer on display.

Think about the anger, the frustration, the pain and the disruption that you feel – the stop and start syndrome that is occasioned by the Referee's whistle that tells you of a foul having been committed.

That is the same cause and effect of the Quotation Marks as they exist wherever they are.

When a goal is scored, of course, we all expect to hear the whistle. Or when the ball goes offside – out of play and out of the football pitch, which full stops, normal comas, question marks and exclamation signs represent, and so are upheld here.

# APPRECIATION

I am grateful to Miss Mavis Abiye Jack and Miss Chioma Judith Nwakuma for the great job they did for me in typing and re-typing the Manuscript that led to the finished product of JJC.

I am also grateful to Godswill Udeme Ikpe for his IT support which led to the Retrieval of a Document and Manuscript once thought to be lost, and to Amenjiba Rose Robert Ibani for being a part of the recovery Team and for the few rework that had to be done to bring back JJC to life!

I am grateful to all my passionate friends who stayed away from me for different reasons which gave me the space and the time that I very badly needed and need to do what I did to bring JJC and others like him to the public.

I am grateful to all those who I may perceive wrongly or rightly as persons who hate me, but through whose hate, and sometimes through whose wish or desire for to kill me disguised as love that I see through, anyway, I received greater insight and understanding of the concept of hate, Dei Gracia, in order for love to be more meaningful to me than I knew and would have known that it is…

**DUMO KAIZER J ORUOBU**
**December 1, 2017, Port Harcourt, NIGERIA.**

# DEDICATION

I dedicate JJC to my friends
*Ekine Ombo Tom Big Harry
*Golden Cyril Gman Dapper
*Edison Amachree
*Okriye Quaje Harry
*Basoene Abbiye-Suku, Ph.D
*Rosetta George Da-Wariboko, Ph.D
*Jahaziel Anapunam Marchie
*Edward Nwosu
*Christopher Ositadinma Nwokwu
*Asikiya Asano Egerton KariibiOmoni
*Charles Awoala Briggs, Ph.D
*Christian Ajoku
*Blessing Didia
*Onyee Nwankpa, Ph.D
*Sylvanus Amah
*Ebenezer Amah
*Basoene Douglas
*Teinye Douglas
*Mpaka Gogo Abite
*Otonye Robert LongJohn

And to God Almighty The I Am That I Am for enabling me to do it as He has done in everything that I have done and will do all my life through, with thanks giving, love and adoration.

# CHAPTER ONE

# PROLOGUE

# WHAT GRAMMARIANS CALL EXTRAPOLATION

We can tell when a man a or woman has bought their very first car, from those who have counted one or more of those four tyre land craft, and are still counting.

They will keep a constant eye on the machine. They will come out from their sitting rooms or bedrooms to take a good look at it, just to make sure that it has not disappeared.

They tiptoe out of meetings or gatherings, no matter how important they are, to go and steal a look at it where it is parked to reassure themselves that it is still there – still there where it is parked.

They would re-park it every so often if other cars parked near theirs are removed, and they felt that those other parking spaces were either more secure, but usually, more exposed than their space for everyone around to see the latest four legs in town and to admire them.

No private conversation would ever be complete or meaningful if they did not create an opportunity to talk about cars – cars just cars, or the beauty, configuration and behaviour of cars, models, brands, colours, anything so long as it is about cars.

They would be most generous in offering to give someone who had no car a ride, no matter how inconvenient taking them to their destinations would be to them. They become best of Neighbours and their brother's or sister's keepers all of a sudden.

They would display all the wonderful facilities on the dashboard – turn on the radio, go from station to station in a mad hurry or play music most times very loudly, to prove how strong the broadcast signals were, and turn on the air conditioner even if the journey were lasting just one minute, or the weather were feverish cold as in winter or a biting harmattan.

They would wash the car at least two times every day, by themselves, no matter how many other relatives or friends request to assist them in doing the bathing. The volunteer helpers could do damage to something on the very expensive car inadvertently, especially if these helpers have bought one before.

They would buy very expressive and expensive car covers which they would take off and put back over it now and again to make sure that nothing had gone amiss, and, sometimes, to make sure that Visitors who might not know the new owner, would know them, and marvel at their latest achievement.

They would hover around the car now and again, wondering where they could drive to, and make very senseless trips, just to reassure themselves that for real, those machines were theirs, and were at their beck and call.

They would follow all the procedures in the manuals and advices given to them for them to deploy before starting the engines – the engine oil check (which they would ask someone who knew better than them to help do for them because they were not conversant with the manuals to read the gauge correctly yet), the water in the Radiator, the seat belt – the A to Z of the Art, Science and Technology of good driving or hitch-free motoring.

Strange, isn't it? Strange, indeed, that as these same religious addicts to best practices mature and later to pale or transit from green to yellow to become Masters of the craft, many an engine catch a fire while in motion on the highways as a result of the engine oil not having been checked properly and topped as appropriate before the journeys were started.

In the same way as we can tell the man or the woman becoming the owner of a car for the very first time, as set out above we can also tell very reasonably correctly, many a man or a woman doing anything for the very first time in their lives – if we pay attention to them and what they display in their affected exterior.

Transfer all the actions of the new car owner from the foregoing to anything else to any circumstance – what grammarians call extrapolation and you will find that they all nearly follow about the same principle.

Anything, including the birth of a baby, or anyone unfortunately experiencing the death of a very close relation or loved one for the very first time.

# CHAPTER TWO

# I HAVE ARRIVED

Jide reached for his winter suit as soon as he received the invitation via the hotel intercom for him to join his colleagues in the lounge bar downstairs. He took great care to make sure he was quite prepared for the day. As a result, he spent a little extra time making sure he wore his warm clothing correctly. He wanted to make sure the clothing fitted perfectly and did what it was expected to do.

It did. It warmed him as he took the staircase instead of the elevator. Bimbo, his compatriot and chaperone, the go-go girl was the first to see him, panting for breath and sweating. 'Ah, Jide, you're sweating this early morning,' she said, almost screaming.

Jide was confused. He did not know the importance of what she said or how to respond. He had to say something anyway. This was something he knew very well because his aunt had persistently drummed it into him back home many moons ago. *Better to say something when someone tells you something or asks you a question, even if you did not quite understand what you were told or asked.* Yes, even if only to keep you from being completely mute. Silence can be interpreted in many, sometimes unintended, ways. Yes, Aunty Omagbemi drummed that into the ears of every child she mentored. And it was on record that nobody ever deviated from it. Jide knew.

'Bim O,' he said, wearing a confused smile, *'Shemo?'* In Yoruba, *Shemo* meant, 'You know, don't you?'

Bimbo immediately screamed, *'Mi mo oo oo'*; 'I know.'

'Goodness,' the silent recorder of every conversation that took place said, looking away. What did Jide want or expect Bimbo to know? And what was she telling him that she knew which he did not know?

When everyone had sat down, their steaming hot breakfasts in front of them, Bimbo, sitting next to Jide, reached for the zipper at the top of his fur coat. Systematically, she disrobed him, whispering softly in his left ear, 'You don't need this on now.'

*'Esee jaare,'* Jide said in Yoruba again. 'Thank you, indeed.' He tried very hard to put up a face appropriate to his moment of near outrage before their coloured colleagues at the breakfast table.

'Next time, Jide,' Bimbo said as they left the table to go to the grocery stand nearby, 'when we plan to go anywhere inside or outside the hotel, please enquire from me what you need to take with you and how you need to dress. *Shoo gbo o,'* she asked him, meaning, 'I hope you heard.'

She had observed—sometimes with pity, sometimes with pain and outrage, and sometimes with abject frustration—how Jide was lost in his wonder at the things he was seeing for the very first time in this strange land. He had become absent-minded and grasped whatever she told him only after she had painstakingly repeated it many times.

She was desirous of making sure he understood what she asked him. That was better than for her to be thoroughly embarrassed by the reactions of their white folks, who saw them as no better than the animals they kept as pets.

'*Daadani,*' he thundered. 'Very well, indeed.' He nodded his oblong head to assure her that he understood what she told him.

He looked very happy and excited. How wonderful to be where he was. And how wonderful—how stupendous—to have Bimbo with him. *What would it have been like were she not there with me?* he wondered, thanking God for his luck.

*England,* he shouted gleefully inside him. *Here I am, marching on your sands. Marching on your belly, back, or on your head with my own legs!* Olonwun Oba mi—*great God, my king,* osheei, *thank you.*

'Now, Jide', Bimbo called him, 'when you go back to your room, please drop the coat. We will not be needing it since the class is inside this building. If we must go out, they will give us notice. And we will also be given sufficient time to go and get ready.'

Jide heard Bimbo loudly and clearly, and did as she said. After God Almighty—whose benevolence, blessings, and favours had made it possible for Aunty Omagbemi to sponsor his fairy-tale trip to this land of many people's dreams—he considered Bimbo next in importance. She was very important in his life. And here she was, the only person he could see who affected his life every hour that ticked by. He had no reason to doubt whatever she told him. As young as she was, Bimbo had been in this land and in other ones like it, places he only heard about as if they were dreamlands, many times before. Yet Bimbo was almost five years younger than him.

One evening after the last of the Course Exercises that they were required to do were done and over with, Bimbo asked Jide to take a walk with her into the streets of Brighton. He was exceedingly thrilled to oblige her.

Bim O oooo! He screamed to hail her. You are such a fantastic planner of events. You know that I have always pleaded with you to take me out into the town so that I can sample what there are out there!

I know. She said. You know too that I always asked you to be patient, and that there is time for everything. I knew that we would go out, but I had to make sure that the timing was right too. Now that our Programme is running to an end, this is the perfect opportunity. After today, we will look for another opening to go shopping for a few things – things for ourselves and things that we will give to members of our families and friends – certain good friends, you know?

Sisi miii! Jide shouted at hearing Bimbo say what she had just said to him, calling her his elder sister now in the heat of his passion to go out – a Lady older than him and superior in his ranking even to Omagbemi his Aunt at that material time. That was what sisi miii was intended to convey.

Are you a Native Doctor who you have the ability to read a person's mind too? He asked her, his two hands on his hips. Ah! I have always wanted to suggest to you that you should take me out for me to see their market. God bless you my sister! God bless you! You are very thoughtful.

Amii! Amii! Bimbo said, Amii meaning Amen. They have two big Fast Food Stores here – one is indigenous and the other one is foreign. Kenturky Fried Chicken is British while McDonald's is Uncle Sam's that is all over the world. They call them outlets as well as Food chains.

Ah! Bimo oo oo! Which one is Uncle Sam? And is he there in our country too? I have not seen him anywhere in it before. Jide said, looking in his compatriot's eyeballs impatient for her to unravel one more mystery for him to learn from in his first appearance in the closest place to Heaven that he knew.

Jide. Bimbo said without displaying any emotions. Uncle Sam is America. It is not a man. Any time you hear someone call Uncle Sam know that they are talking about the United States of America. It is the short form of United and States called together. U for Uncle which is the United bit, and S for Sam which is the letter representing States. Don't forget this. People will laugh at you if you ask them what Uncle Sam means. There is no McDonald's in our country. Kentucky is not there too. Maybe one day they will consider it expedient to come and open some outlets in our big Cities.

Thank you very much big sissy for telling me. Jide said. Which one are we going to visit today? Is it Uncle – Uncle Sam or the other one? What do you say the other one is called? He asked her looking confused.

KFC. Bimbo said. It is called KFC for short – Kentucky Fried Chicken. We can visit all of them today. It doesn't take time. And they are usually not far from each other because of their cut throat competition. We can spend twenty minutes in one and another twenty minutes or so in the other. Where you like one much more than the other we can decide to spend more time there than the one that you find less interesting.

I am in heaven already! Jide told Bimbo. This is pure Heaven!

They decided to stay longer at the McDonald's than at the KFC for many considerations. Jide said since his country men and women preferred imported goods to home made products they should give greater attention to McDonald's than they should give to KFC because McDonald's was foreign where they were in England – yes, McDonald's was an import from America or uncle Sam here in England. And because that was the case, and because he had also been told before that America was a much bigger country than Britain and much more sophisticated than nearly every other country in the world, they should pay premium to the Burgers of McDonald's. He and Bimbo were in the Queen's England, afterall, and, therefore, they can visit a KFC outlet here whenever they desired to do so. That was their third reason, which, taken together with their other reasons, made a lot of sense to the two visitors from Will Rock, former Colony of Imperial Britain, England or the United Kingdom.

Jide took in as much of what he heard and saw as he possibly could within the time at his disposal, wondering at every turn and twist or at every twist and turn what America or Uncle Sam would look like, if, as people say, it was much more sophisticated than England, with all the near impossible advancements and out of the world scientific attractions that he was seeing where he was – this place where he had been during his nearly two weeks of stay studying in the most friendly environment he had ever seen.

Bimbo advised him to keep his voice down as they talked while waiting for the foods and drinks that they had ordered to be served.

When he asked her why she said so, she was also very quick to tell him that unlike Will Rock where they came from, especially unlike in their own part of that country where people were very well known to be very loud in expressing themselves at gatherings, here, people valued silence as much as they valued their privacies and saw loud people as uncouth and constituting a nuisance to others.

They would brand him as a bush man if they heard him talk as loudly as they did back home. She told him matter of factly.

Jide believed Bimbo. He believed her because apart from the noise of china wares that he could hear as forks and knives made hurried contacts with the food inside them and as the foods disappeared into the mouths of those sitted all around and the occasional guffaws and hilarious laughters of the merry eaters of the delicious meals, he did not hear anyone expressing themselves with the kind of loudness that he was used to in Ocean View City in Will Rock, especially among his Egba people.

Will I ever get the opportunity to visit that Egbon? Jide asked Bimbo as they walked out of the KFC outlet to look for a Bus on which to ride back to their Hotel. Egbon was Yoruba to indicate an older brother or sister or any relation older than the speaker whether feminine or masculine in gender.

Visit which Egbon? Bimbo asked him, wondering who he was talking about.

She ei you said people call that place Uncle Sam, didn't you say so? He asked her. Didn't you say that the man there is called Uncle Sam? He repeated with emphasis.

Ah-ah-ah-ah-ah-ah! Jide! Don't kill me with laughter oooo! She said wobbling with uncontrollable laughter. Egbon, indeed. She added after she pulled herself back on track from the brink. Did you know in advance that you were going to come to England one year ago? She asked him.

One year ke? Jide asked her, ke meaning Are you kidding? And went on to tell her that one year was too long a time for her to refer to in making her point. I did not know even three days before we travelled out that I would ever come here! He added. Don't you remember all the constraints that I faced? He asked her. Tell me what you are telling me *Ojare* – meaning please or my dear, indicating the listener's appreciation of what he is being told.

Good. Bimbo said. Very good. The same way as you did not know that you would ever come here, and you are here now, you would also not know when you will get there! That is how God works. Only He knows the destinies of every man and every woman and their ultimate destinations in life as we all move along in time and space blindly. Just relax. America is the same distance from here as our country is by air from this place that we are. Before you know it, you are there! Nothing is impossible in this our world, especially if you believe in the awesome might of God.

Very true. He agreed with her. Very true. Nobody can dispute that with you.

Back in the Hotel, Jide persuaded Bimbo to have a drink on him – *real drink*, he called it, since at the KFC they did not sell alcohol which he called ogogoro – ogogoro meaning spirit – any liquor that can intoxicate any consumer but most pungent if that spirit were the product of distilled palm wine also called *Kai-kai* in West Africa but with it's origins from the impossible Will Rock.

The two foreigners spent more time in the bar of their Hotel than they spent outside of it, which in turn also brought with it consequences – consequences not quite intended.

For when Jide guided Bimbo back to her room she asked him to spend a few more moments with her in there than anyone of them intended to spend. And feeling quite tipsy himself, Jide had felt compelled to oblige her in order for him to also reasonably recover from the effect of the ogogoro that she was contending with.

In the end something else happened which none of them had planned that should happen. Something else happened.

Or did it ever cross their minds? There was no way of knowing the truth about that question. Only time answered questions like that. Yes almighty time.

After a spell of three weeks, Jide and Bimbo returned to Ocean View City. Jide had engaged Bimbo in a very spirited conversation throughout the duration of the flight from Oxbow Leg Airport in London to Megida Hassan International Airport in Ocean View City, keeping quiet only when there was turbulence in the air, and at which time Bimbo always took over the conversation, but only in order that she would calm him by asking him to relax and not be afraid, saying that it was normal for them to go through turbulent weather once in a while just as road users encountered bumps and pot holes while driving their cars on the roads and on the Highways anywhere in the world, especially in Southern Will Rock because of the conditions of abject neglect of the roads there.

You have been baptized! Bimbo told him as soon as they got out of the Aircraft, smiling broadly and patting him tenderly on his back.

Baptized ke? Jide asked her, what he said meaning Only baptized?

Kini? She asked him, what she asked him meaning Then what is it if it is not Baptism?

Which Pastor Baptized me? And in which Church, Bi moooo? He asked her, laughing very broadly.

Abejide! Bimbo called his name in full for the first time in a very long while. I mean you have been there and have come back to land. That's what I mean by you have been Baptized. Ah! She screamed in surprise, looking at him askance with a mixture of admiration and disdain.

Moo tide! Mo o tide! Jide screamed, more than amplifying what she had said, what he said meaning I have arrived! I have arrived! I have arrived! He said again and again, proudly flapping his shoulders like a bird about to take flight, and thumping his chest like a Champion Wrestler demonstrating his physical prowess to the excited Spectators to intimidate his opponents.

I have arrived! Yes! Didn't the people of the world say that a man or a woman becomes what they thought they were? He asked himself. Be e ni He said – be e nii meaning That is it! He had joined the club, or if you like, he had become a member of the class of those people who have made it in life! Those who have *been to* as well – those who have travelled Overseas or gone to the magic lands of strange coloured people – white men and white women or red or orange skinned people. More specifically people who have set foot on London soil – London the personification of Overseas and all of it's attributes as far as the Yorubas of the world were concerned.

Bimbo laughed very loudly and boisterously, and for a very long time too. There was nothing strange, surprising or odd in his reactions. She told herself. He was only acting true to type. She said to herself again as Jide basked in his euphoria of his epochal triumphant return back home from England – land of many wonders.

They were almost stepping out into the madness of Ocean View City, after walking past the doors with Something To Declare on the right side, and Nothing to Declare on the left side written very conspicuously.

It would be inappropriate for Abimbola to wickedly or mischievously humour Abejide in the presence of happy family members and friends of theirs – in particular his own friends and family members who could be seen craning their necks anxiously to see him – and anxiously waiting to hug them for their safe return back from abroad – the land of Oyimbo people or white skinned men and women.

She took one quick look at him, placed her right hand on his left shoulder and then in measured tones told him Jide, Ekabo! Ekabo meaning Welcome.

Jide gave her a crushing hug, his thirty two teeth widely on sickening display – a display like those of the killer crocodile hunting flies in his sun bathing past time by the swamps of the mangrove forests.

Next time you go to England or to any land of the Oyimbo, you will not be a JJC anymore! That's what I meant by Baptism. Congrats! Bimbo told him laughing.

Jide chuckled, caught between his concerns for how to make his elegant presence very eventful for the crowd of friends and family waiting for him out there that he could see and what to say to Bimbo or how to very appropriately respond to what she had said to him on these home grounds.

There was not time enough for anyone of them to say anything else.

They were now out of the Arrival Lounge – touts, Drivers and mischief makers all waiting to get the better of any unsuspecting Returnees.

The large crowd of well-wishers had taken over, hugging and kissing them, hugging and kissing Jide more than they did hug and kiss Bimbo the frequent flyer. She had been through this routine many times before.

But unknown to anyone of the people in that happy crowd of well-wishers, including Abejide himself, Bimbo had a problem on her mind – a very serious problem on her mind which was almost shaking her to her very foundations– a problem which she was grappling with an uncomfortable silence in the best way that she could.

# CHAPTER THREE

# AMERICA, HERE I COME!

Now, Jide. Auntie Omagbemi called Abejide one early morning. It is one month since you came back from that place called England or what else, is it not? Good. Still are you saying that we will not hear anything else in this house apart from what you saw there? And you were there for how long? You were there for less than one month. Isn't that true? What would you do or tell us if you had stayed there for one year or for longer? She asked him.

I am very sorry, Auntie miii. I am very sorry. I didn't know that you were behind me and hearing what I was telling them. He said.

Good. The Bread winner of the home said. Now you know that I am here. So let us hear other things apart from England, English men and women and their foolish ways.

I hear, Ma. He said. I am very sorry once again.

Jide was shocked by his Aunt's description of the wonderful people he had seen in Brighton and London as people with very foolish ways. If those near Angels on Earth were foolish in any way, then what was she going to describe her own people here, including he himself? What about she herself? Or could she be of the opinion that she was the only wise person here? He could not understand. He would ask her someday – yes, someday, at a very auspicious or propitious moment why she described the English people the way she just did.

Auntie Gbemi. Little Sola called Omagbemi the way all of her Dependants called her. Uncle Jide said that throughout his stay in that place, NEPA did not take the light even for one minute. Is it true or uncle was just joking about it with us when he told us that?

Here we go again! The woman said, displaying no emotions whatsoever. Shoo o – Shoo o. She called Sola fondly. You just heard me tell Jide not to talk about England again. And there you are talking about it? Well, since it is a question that you have asked me, and since I am the one who I have always told you to speak up any time that any one says something to you, I will answer you. I will answer you. But as I said I don't want to hear about England, Brighton or London every moment in this house anymore. Do you hear me? You should all read your books very well, pass your exams and go to England yourselves, as well as to France, Germany, Italy, Canada and America. Live and work there if you have the opportunity to go there. And send me Dollars from there every time you have the opportunity to do so.

All the people in the sitting room clapped and said Amen to what she had said which they all took to be her prayer for all of them to become successful in life.

That is good. Very good. She said in acknowledging their commendable gesture. All of you will go to those lands! All of you saying Amen to what I said, and for clapping too very spontaneously.

God takes records of every good wish that we make to Him. Today He has heard what you have wished and He has taken a record of it. Soon I shall be receiving Pounds Sterling from those of you who go to live and work in England, Dollars from those who go to America and other currencies like French Franc, Euros and Liras from those who will go to other lands of the Oyinbo that Jide never gets tired of talking about. Yes, Sola. Jide is quite right that power supply out there is constant and never interrupted. They don't have NEPA there too. We are the only people who are unfortunate to have our Electricity Supply Company called NEPA which our people have interpreted in many ways-*Never Expect Power Always. Power Holding Company* – Not Power Supplying Company. *PHCW PLC – Power Holding Company of Will Rock, Please Light Candle.* These are some names that they call our Electricity Supply Companies here. There in England, America or anywhere else outside our country – even in neighbouring Ghana and Togo or the Republic of Benin next door to us, they do not have NEPA. What they have are Electricity Providing Organizations that are alive to their responsibilities which they see as civic and obligatorily mandatory and not just work which they do any how they like just to be paid a salary. It is a part and parcel of the ethos of their national life. Well, I am sorry to be speaking big, big Grammar, Sola. Ethos means their way of life. There is nothing like Power failure there. You will experience it yourself when you go there. She said. You will go there very soon and see it yourself.

So, Auntie, why can't we have the same thing here? Sola asked her.

Good question. Very good question. She said. That will be for another day, Sho-shooo. To answer that question meaningfully will take me a minimum of five hours. And I don't have that time right now. Let everyone please go inside and get themselves busy. I need to cook some food for us to eat.

Everyone got up from where they had been sitting and went about helping the Bread Winner of the House to do what she had told them that she needed to do– prepare food for the family to eat.

Poor Sola. She muttered to herself as she lit the gas in the kitchen. Maybe things will change in his generation. Maybe in his time. Do we have a Government here? We don't. And why is that the case? Why is that our lot? Why we are so blessed by God Almighty and yet are so cursed by our own people – our own people who call themselves Leaders? What are they leading? Who are they leading? They should come here and tell my little son Sola whether it is true that in England Nepa does not cut power supply. And why here Nepa means something completely different – an Organization that condemns us to darkness and makes us deaf with the sounds of the generators of those who can afford them.

It was a Saturday morning that moved quickly to early afternoon. After her cooking was over and the family of seven sat to eat what looked like a combination of breakfast and lunch, the Matriarch found it necessary to address the enquiry of little Sola's.

I am breaking my own rule here for people eating food, especially food with pepper – plenty of pepper in it not to talk while eating, to talk to all of you because of what Shooo Shoo o asked me earlier in the day – his question which forced me to the kitchen in the end. And I am addressing that his question because no matter how I try to run away from answering it, it will not go away. If I am the one who taught you to never keep silence if anyone says anything to you, I should not be the one to also do the opposite of what I want you to do as a precept or should I call it habit? She asked herself.

Lady Omagbemi wiped the sweat on her forehead with the napkin she held in her left hand and drank a bit of the fresh fruit juice in the large jug in front of her.

Jide was right when he told you that Nepa does not cut power supply in England. The only time that you will experience what they call power outage there is if there is a very serious natural disaster.

If there happens to be an Earthquake, for instance which, as you know, is rare except in Japan where it occurs quite frequently. Or if there is an accident that leads to power cables being broken or uprooted by accident. Even at such emergencies, first of all they will inform the people about what has actually happened. They will tell the people what they are doing to make sure that power is restored and how long it will take for that to happen. And at exactly the time that they have said that that will happen, power will be restored, most times even before the time that they had announced.

Here if we are unfortunate to have such an emergency, only those in the place or vicinity of that accident happening will also know about it. The rest of the people of the country will be kept in the dark while they will take no action to repair the damage. Then you wonder if we all belong to the same human race. And our leaders are always going to those countries for their holidays and other businesses almost every day. They buy everything that has a name there – from electronics to toilet paper and bring back home with them at the end of those their visits. They buy everything and bring back - everything from cars to toys for their children. What they do not see there to bring back with them here is the power supply that is steady. The gutters that are kept clean every day. They do not see the bus and train transportation services that work like the clock. They come back to the filth that they left here. And how do they end? What happens when their tenures are over? Many of them end up in jail for frauds that are uncovered shortly after they leave or however long it takes for those sordid deeds to be unearthed. Many years ago this was what led to soldiers always taking over power through what they call coups – military coups through which they told us that they would correct the misgovernments of the civilian administrations. Now we do not know anymore which one is better than the other between Military Government and Civilian Government. One word defines all of them– Corruption. Corruption which is like a foundation on which all our other problems are built. Maybe all that will change when Sola becomes a Governor, and maybe President later? Isn't that possible? It is possible. Maybe only when people of Sola's age bracket will be in charge of the administration of our country after they have been to England and to America and come back with all the good things that they will see there to do them here instead of coming back with toilet papers and can beer. Ah! Nobody has been eating their food? Let me stop here. Please eat your food. As for me, talking about these things takes my appetite away. I cannot eat anymore now. Eat, eat, eat and put away your plates. She said as she rose from her chair. She was going into her room to brood over the oddities of life here in her country.

Auntie please come and eat some food from my plate. You must be hungry. Sola said. She was struck as with a spear. She stood for a long moment and reflected on what to do in response to that request.

Thank you, my dear. She told Sola and walked over to his side. Aren't you very kind and considerate? Let me see how your food tastes. Maybe it is even tastier than my own. Mmmm! She exclaimed and pouted loudly. It tastes wonderful! She said and patted the little boy on his back very tenderly as she walked away from him in the direction that she was going when he called her.

Sola looked at his Auntie, speechless. What a pleasurable woman she is. He thought. And how kind and loving. He cast occasional glances at his other relations at the table and smiled victoriously.

He would be a Governor of this State. He would also become the President of the country! Then he would make sure that Nepa does not take electricity power away from them. He would make sure that there was power supply always. He thought believing that it will come through very soon. Yes, very soon.

11

# CHAPTER FOUR

# THE SHADOWS OF BRIGHTON

That is why. That is why I called you to meet me here so that I can tell you – tell you what has happened without anyone around us to inhibit any one of us from our reactions and utterances. Bimbo said, trying very hard not to look at Jide as she spoke.

Now. Bi moo. Jide said after a very long silence during which he shed tears just as Bimbo herself cried throughout her narration. Who else knows about this? He asked her.

My brother in the US. She said. My older brother in America, Olufemi. He is the closest person to me in all my world.

And what did he say when he heard what you told him? Jide asked Bimbo.

That is a very good question. She said. I was not surprised at what he said. He had always wanted for me to bear a child, married or not married, but preferably if I were properly married. He says he is very happy. And he also wants me to come over to him as quickly as possible before anyone else finds out here that I am pregnant. That's the kind of sweetheart that he is to me. If everyone were like him – if everyone in my life were like him, I would have no problems whatsoever.

That is wonderful. Jide said, wiping the tears falling off from his cheek. Now what do you yourself feel like? What do you want to do? He asked her.

I don't know if I understand you very well. I doubt it if I understand what you mean by your two questions. What do I feel like? What do I want to do? I have already told you what I have been asked to do –to travel to America as soon as possible. How I feel? That is the question that I do not know how to answer. You know that what happened on that night was purely an accident. I say so because I do not believe that even you yourself planned for what happened to happen. And I should not blame you. You were on your way out going back to your room when I called you back to stay some more with me. So I should blame myself, not you. Afterall you are a man who you also have feelings. What I don't know is Do I want to have you as my husband even if you tell me that you want me to be your wife? And two. If you say that I should be your wife, would I be willing to be your wife? Would you yourself want to have me as your wife on your own, whether we call what has happened an accident or not? That is how I feel. That is how I feel. Now you know. Now you know, don't you? She asked Jide bluntly.

I know. I know. Jide said, looking across her forehead, quite confused.

And then he kept quiet for a very long time. When he spoke again later, what he told her shocked her to her foundations once again.

You know, Bi moo oo. He started. You know that you are a natural Adviser. That is what you are that I knew you to be even before we travelled together to England three months ago. And because of the trust that I have grown to have in you, you will believe me too when I tell you that if what has happened between us now happened between me and someone else, and I asked you for advice, you will give me the very best advice that anyone can give me. Therefore, it is still the same you who I have to ask in our present situation to please advise me exactly the way that you will advise me if you were not the person involved with me in the present circumstance.

But I am involved. Bimbo retorted almost before he finished speaking those words. I am the one involved with you in this situation, so it is difficult for me to detach myself from what I should say to you as advice. You should, therefore, please go ahead to share your own ideas with me. If I find them to be okay and good enough, I will tell you so. Where I do not think that what you share with me as your own ideas are not okay, I will then tell you what I have on my mind so that we can reach a decision together. Bimbo said.

To be honest with you, Bimbo. Jide said. To be very candid and honest with you, I have no ideas in my head at all as I sit here with you on what I should say. It never crossed my mind at all that this could happen. As for you, you knew about it maybe a little more than two months ago, and, therefore, must have also formed some mental pictures in your head or mind – ideas as to what you would like to do about it. Share those thoughts with me please so that I can think along those lines that you will proffer both as advice and as a solution.

Jide. Bimbo said. I want what you tell me to come straight from you. Straight from your own heart without it being influenced or coloured by anything that anyone else or I should say. I will allow you to think about it for as long as you will want to think about what to say. For as long as you will want to consider what you will want to say, but please not longer than necessary because we have to reach a decision as soon as possible in order that I do not become the subject or object of lousy and idle gossips and fire side stories when people begin to see my transformation from the lizard that I am looking like now into something like a pot-bellied consumer of large quantities of beer very soon.

I understand. Jide said. I quite understand. When did you tell your brother that you will call him back to give him information on what you will want to do? He asked her. Bimbo heaved a sigh and breathed hard.

My brother and I talk any time we desire to talk to each other, notwithstanding what we all know now. That does not matter in how long it takes you to let me know what you think you should do. She said.

Bi moo oo. Jide said, his mood looking cloudy. I don't want to say that First of all I am sorry about what has happened. I don't want to say so. If I should be honest and truthful to you and to myself, what I should tell you and let the whole wide world to also know, is that I am very happy – very happy that I am on the road to becoming a father! Yes! That I am on the road to becoming a father for the very first time in my life, and that that fatherhood apart, the child is coming from a mother – from a woman who any Prince or King in the whole world would want to have as their wife – you Bimbo! And that is where my problem lies. That is where my problem is because the way that I am right now, the important question that is there for me to ask myself and to answer myself very honestly is Can I measure up to that expectation – can I truthfully measure up to you? Do I have all that it will take for me to make you proud of also becoming the first time mother that you are about to become? That is the problem that I am facing.

13

Jide, stop there! Bimbo said, touching him on his lips as if she were asking her fingers to act the words that she had just spoken for her. Life does not exist on the basis of the equality of the men and women of the world in any relationship. If anything, life is exactly the opposite of that. Life is here in existence – the existence that we stay in and pass through because no two people are exactly the same. To make me proud because of how much money you can invest in me now should not be your immediate concern or worry at this time of near emergency. That time belongs in the future – the future which also belongs to God and not to any one of us humans. All that you are required to do now is to own up to the responsibility that we have on our hands, even though I am the one who I am carrying that problem in my womb right now if I should call it a problem. And we can go on from there. That's all I want to hear from you for now. That you accept the responsibility that I am carrying – Jide, that you are responsible for it. That's all.

I wish that that is all that I need to do. Jide said, shaking his head. How I wish that that is all that I need to do – to say that I accept the responsibility – that I am responsible for it as simply as you have made it sound like. You know, Bimbo, that if there is anything which will make me happy in this my world, that thing is for me to be close to you – for me to be very close to you! Don't you know? Don't you know? Especially after that life time that we spent together there in England? That is the truth. And I am sure that you know. I am sure that you know this to be true as much as I know. Why should I, therefore, have any problems with the great opportunity that I now have of my having to have you become a permanent feature in my space – for you, Bimbo, to become a permanent presence in my life? I should not have any problems about that becoming a reality without my having to spend a fortune for it to happen. Ah! Bimbo! Ah! How I wish I had a fortune – a fortune to spend – to lavish on you! How I wish!

Ah! Olonwun! God! What's wrong with you, Jide? Bimbo screamed. What has fortune got to do with me an ordinary girl who I am the way that I am that you can see that I am? What has fortune got to do with what we have been talking about? Okay! Okay! Jide, you wanted to hear from me what I would advise you if I were not the person involved in what the matter is that we have been discussing. Just tell the lady concerned, Jide, that you love her! Jide, just tell the lady that you love her! That will be enough! Come to think of it, Jide. Have you ever told me that you love me? She asked him and then folded her arms around her breasts and also crossed her legs as she sat where she was sitting.

I am very sorry, Bimbo, that I have not said that to you before. I am very sorry. Please believe me. Please believe me that I am sorry. I always came very close to saying it. Very close to saying it, but I was afraid to say it. I was afraid to say it because I wondered what I should do with myself if you turned me down as soon as I said it. The truth, dear mother of my son, is that I love you! Ah! Did I say son? What if all of a sudden I become father of a son and a daughter – a set of bouncing twins all at once? What did I say? Father of a son? One child? No. I mean father of a set of twins!

Bimbo sprang up to her feet shouting Jide! That is the truth! I am carrying a boy and a girl! That's what the Doctors told me when I went there to them for them to carry out tests for us to be certain about my condition. Jide! Are you also a Prophet? Ah! Jide! Are you also a Prophet? Because that is the truth! I am carrying a set of twins in my womb as I sit here! That is the gospel truth!

The two people held themselves tight, shivering for a very long time, with excitement, happiness and fears of the unknown – apparent fears about the unknown as far as Abejide was concerned, their heartbeats almost audible to them.

When they broke free from their frenetic embrace, they not only felt relieved, they also began to feel that they now belonged to each other, and, therefore, would do anything and everything that they did from that time on with the other person's feelings, interests and gains taken into consideration in whatsoever it was that they did. They should take everyone that they held dear in their lives into confidence about what had developed between them without delay to avoid any backlashes. Bimbo would be bound for Uncle Sam in the next one month or as soon as she received the American Visa. Jide should join her there as soon as he could, but not later than three months after her own arrival. They would have a very modest wedding ceremony within the sophisticated bowel of Uncle Sam before the arrival of the twins who would be called Jide and Bimbo Junior.

The two Lovers gave themselves a big hug once again and headed in different directions to their places of abode happy and satisfied with the turn of events.

Auntie Omagbemi could not believe her ears after Jide broke the news to her on his arrival back home.

How come all that you ever told us – I should say all that you ever told me, Jide. Lady Omagbemi asked her Nephew, looking at him with apparent pleasure after hearing from him what he told her. Is how Nepa never goes to bed in England and stories about an evening in which the two of you went hunting for Burgers and for Chickens, and not anything near the meat of the real story of how the night wrapped up? Aren't you a master of suspense, Jide? Or were you, as they say, saving the best for last? Either way you have been wonderful, my dear son. Omagbemi said. You have proved yourself to be a Master of suspense drama, and to be very patient and calculating.

You know, Auntie mi ii. Jide said, looking away from the woman sitting majestically in front of him. That I cannot discuss such things with you. Ah! Auntie! For me to tell you such a thing! Wouldn't you think that I have gone mad? Ah! Auntie mii!

I know, Jide. She said. I know. You have been extremely respectful. You have been such a respectful and wonderful little brother of mine. Now you are going to be a father. Father of beji – twins! Congratulations! Congratulations also for your trip to Uncle Sam that is coming very soon! Nothing will stop that from happening by the special Grace of God Almighty.

Amen! Thank you very much, my dear Auntie. Jide said looking very sober. Some mothers haven't done for their Children what you have done for me and have been doing for me all my life. God bless you! Jide told the completely relaxed woman as their late night conversation came to a very happy end.

# CHAPTER FIVE

# IS THIS YOU, UNCLE SAM?

What are you going to do there – do you want to tell me – aah! Jaideei?

The Lady at the Visa section of the American Embassy at Eagle Crescent asked Abejide as he stared at her as though he were dreaming.

I am going to marry. He said.

Going to marry in the States? The Lady asked him in utter disbelief and surprise.

Yes! He said beginning to brighten up. He was sure that she was happy with what he had told her.

Just a second. His Interviewer said and rushed off into the adjoining room. When she returned the smile on her face was gone. In it's place was hurry and impatience – the usual impatience of a typical white woman with a typical black man even in the black man's own country.

Now what you are saying is that you are going to the States only to look for a woman to marry? And how long do you think that is going to take you? She asked him.

My wife is already there. She is there already. Jide said shouting.

Who's there? The woman you're going to get married to or your wife? She asked him.

My wife is there already. He said again looking very sure of what he had said.

Is she American or English? The Lady asked him.

She speaks English. Jide answered.

I mean is she an American or an English woman? She asked him.

Bimbo is from here. She is from Will Rock. He said thumbing down.

O she's a Will Rocker? The Visa Officer asked him.

Yes, Ma. She is Yoruba like me.

Oka yi! The Lady said, dragging the pronunciation of the word okay to the limit, startling Jide in the process. Now, what's she doing out there? Does she have a green card? She asked Jide. Has she gaat a green card?

Her Passport is green – yes, the same colour as my own Passport. Yes, she has a green passport. He said.

I know that your Passport is green in colour. The American Lady said. But what I'm asking you is different from the colour of your Passports. Is she working in the States? The woman that you say you want to marry – Armeeen, eeshee wekking there? She screamed in typical American parlance, looking impatient.

No, Ma! Jide answered. Only her brother is working. He added.

I see. The Lady said, looking pensive. So her braather's gaat a green card?

I don't know. Jide said. What is green card if it is not the colour of the Passport? He asked her in surprise.

I'm sorry you didn't know. The Lady said. Do you know how long her brother has been there? She asked him.

Yes, Ma. He said. He has been there for more than ten years.

Ten years? She asked more as a rhetorical than as a question put to him. That's okaiyi! She added and then disappeared into the adjoining room again.

Congratulations, Jaidei! She told him when she came back the second time, handing his Passport back to him with her left hand. You've been granted a Visa for one year! Enjoy yourself and your wedding! She added, smiling.

Thank you, Ma! Thank you very much! Jide said. And he sprang from where he was and walked away, not believing his luck.

Uncle Sam! He shouted once he was out of earshot of the Lady. Here I come to you! Olonwun Oba – God The King! Osheei! Thank you. He sang as he strolled away.

Madam Omagbem Isola Fadeyi was exceedingly happy that Abejide was able to secure the American Visa almost completely unaided – unaided by Earth, Wind or Fire. She could also not believe that he was granted a Visa that had a lifespan of one Calendar year. She would be happy even if they had given him a Visa for not more than six months. What she prayed for was for three or four months just so that he could pull away the wedding ceremony in Georgia's Atlanta City and return home to Will Rock. Now, happy as she was at the turn of events, she was troubled at heart because she knew that she faced a challenge – a challenge to surmount and for which she must also talk to Bolaji Oladimeji once again – once again after all the favours that he had done her and after all the things that he had pulled off for her in the last five years since the death of her husband – Chief Oniru Olagbegi his childhood friend and class-mate. Not that those favours were altogether free. No. The Americans are damn right when they say that There is no free lunch. Yes. They are right. There is no free Lunch, not only in America, their America but anywhere in the whole wide world.

How Omagbemi wished that Abejide knew what was going through her mind. How she wished that he knew. What a shame. She thought. That there was no way she could tell him what that rush of clouds – those passing of clouds of different shades and configurations in her mind were or anything near what she harboured on her mind. She remembered the last time that the man was here on the grounds of their house. How Abejide was running from pillar to post and from posts to pillars in his frantic – his frenetic and determined excitement to do all of their biddings – to do whatsoever she and Bolaji wanted for him to do for them. How the man Omo Bolaji himself had grown to like Jide – Jide who he called Bejide in his usual slant that was different from Jide or Abejide that nearly everyone else called him, with an unusual passion. Which is a very good thing. A very good thing. She told herself now. Yes. It is a very good thing when someone who you have warmed into, especially in these her circumstances here – yes, when someone you have warmed into themselves have someone else who they in turn can also warm into that makes everyone involved in – And then she broke off. She broke off from her train of thought to question herself in what she was about to say. In what? Ah Olonwun! Isn't it a crime of a sort? Misdemeanour, impropriety or faux pas – anything which anyone does only in secret, is it not a crime? She asked herself again. Yes. Yes … Yes. She continued. If there is someone else they can warm into in what they were engaged in, in cahoots or in whatsoever manner. It is good that it is about Jide or Bejide that I am going to ask him to do something of great importance for me again.

Auntie. Jide called her after waiting for her to speak to him for a very long time and not hearing her say anything. Let me run to the place that you said that I should go. Or should I hang on some more? He asked her.

Ah! Omomi ii – She cut him short, Omomi ii meaning my dear child, the dear sounding particularly endearing in this instance – exceedingly endearing.

Not yet. Don't go yet. She said looking uncertain. I am still trying to figure out something. Don't worry. I will have to go by myself. But I have to call him on the phone first. Well done. Well done. I have to do everything that I can to solve it. It is something that I must do. And I must not fail.

The two people all retired into the Apartment, America at the heart of their thoughts, but each one of them worrying about the same trip to America or Uncle Sam differently.

There was a fairly long telephone conversation between the Matriarch of the home and someone far away from that home. Soon, thereafter, the Lady was on her way out into the City. No good thing comes to you where you are sitting down or standing. You have to go in search of it with your legs. Yes, with your legs, and many times with much more than your legs.

You've not looked this distraught ever since I have known you, Ggbemi. Bode observed the mood of the Lady who had made his emergency presence where they were possible, almost at the snap of her fingers as soon as he sat down beside her on the massive three sitter.

I may look as unhappy as you have observed. She told him, barely looking at him. But one thing is also certain and sure. And that is that your presence here with me has brought me great joy. I am immensely grateful to God Almighty and to you that you are here. Here with me. Believe me I am happy.

You must believe me that I am happy.

Bode held her close to him. And she reciprocated by holding on to him too. He took one more step. And she reciprocated too. And that went on and on until there was nothing more for either of them to initiate for the other to reciprocate.

There was no doubt anymore on the mind of anyone of them that what Omagbemi had spoken about in the beginning was the truth. The truth that no matter her outward looks, Bode's presence was joy to her for which she was immensely grateful to God Almighty and to Bode himself.

Omaanmi ii. Bode called softly to her as he cuddled her like a little baby, Omaami ii meaning my Omagbemi.

She turned slowly to her left to steal a look at his face with the sweat cascading down from it.

Bode my all. She called him, holding him tighter than before, shivering involuntarily out of her sheer exhaustion and great emotional release and relief occasioned by what they had been through during the past moments.

Isn't it a mystery how this thing works? He asked her. Isn't it a mystery that two completely different people – two adults like us set in our various ways can without any elaborate planning and all the things that go into the intricate process of decision making still submerge into each other so perfectly and as automatically as we have done, that it is almost as if we planned it together ages ago?

I agree with you. She said, maintaining her hold on him. I agree with you. That is what it is. And that is why those who have experienced it before us and know it better than us called it love – love which does not die from generation on to succeeding generations.

Omami ii. He whispered very loudly to compliment her for the beauty of her poetry in analyzing what he had said. That is what I miss where I am forced to stay twenty four hours daily. The beauty of your poetry and the lucidity of your thoughts, no matter the subject.

Thank you, Thank you, my love. She said. I believe you now because you have always said so. Thank you.

Now you know that I am a debtor. And, therefore, it is time for me to pay my debt. Bode said peering into her dim eyes.

Debtor, Bode? She asked him, taken completely aback by what he had just said.

Yes, Gbemi. That's what I am. Not only me but any man anywhere in the whole wide world who goes through what I have just gone through here. It is a huge debt which every Gentleman worth his salt or onion must pay without any prompting. Yes, Gbemi. That is the truth that I know. Now what was the cause of your being so troubled that you insisted for us to meet today? That is the debt that I am talking about. Ah, Bola. She screamed in whispers. Was that what you were hinting at? She asked him, turning away from him shyly the way a molusc moved away from stimuli in it's path of movement. Don't you make me look like a whore by that? She asked sighing sadly.

Gbemi, how dare you say that? Ah! He asked in a rush and exclaimed too very racily. My goodness, Gbemi! You make me look like a wretched Soldier in an Army of plunderers fit only for a Court Marshal and the firing squad! How can you call yourself a whore with no one else but me, Bola in your company? Have I not myself become the male version of the same thing?

I am very sorry, Bola. I am sorry. She said. But that is what any woman is who does what I have done with you here if that man is any man except her lawfully wedded husband. There is no escaping from that truth. Not only from the truth inherent in it. There are also consequences, Bola. Consequences. Dire consequences for me and for you too. Which is why we always ask Him for forgiveness every day. And may He please forgive us. Because can we help it? Can anyone help it? Especially someone like me in my situation? She asked as though she were talking to herself.

You are not in any situation, Gbemi, different from a King on his throne or a Queen sitting beside him. The man said. There is none righteous, Gbemi. No, not one! The bible says so. And, therefore, nobody should see themselves as the very worst of sinners anywhere in the whole wide world. Nobody. And God is merciful yet. He is kind. He is understanding. He is merciful. Shake off that dust of guilt, Gbemi and tell me what I have asked of you, let me hear it and address it so that we can go back to our different places of abode whether those places make us happier or not because we have to go back there any way. He said. In conclusion, sadness in his voice which she could feel pungently.

You have spoken well, Bola. You are always very quick to compliment me for what you describe as the poetry of my speech. You do that as a routine yourself, but as often as you do that you also hide the fact that you are yourself the master of that gift that you are all too often quick to ascribe to me. You are a wonderful speech maker. If you doubt it please play back what you just spoke and listen to it yourself and make the judgment yourself. I am sorry if I said the wrong thing or the correct thing the wrong way. Ejooo ma binu – please do not be annoyed. She said.

Then there was a long silence. A very long silence. Each one of them turned over in their minds what they had been through and what they had said to each other, each one of them agreeing with their different positions. Yes. They said to themselves. Friends must tell each other the truth as it is. Friends owe themselves that much as a debt that they must pay as a sacred duty which should also be seen as sacrosanct. They all knew too that they must leave the Guest House environment that they were in, and sooner rather than later.

Lady Omagbemi shared her thoughts with the big time Politician and Technocrat Bolaji on what she wanted him to engineer for Abejide her very obedient and dutiful Nephew as he looked forward to his trip to the United States of America to cut his teeth as a married man and as a prospective father –a first time father.

Bolaji told his Mistress how relieved and yet surprised he was that what she had told him was all that she came to tell him as the problem or burden that she bore that was crushing her. If that was all she was bothered about. He said. They did not need to meet where they met or first of all make themselves guilty as Sinners before arriving at a solution. She should have mentioned it to him on the telephone and he would have taken the same action as he would take now that she had told him about it where they were. Some of the guilt poetry and sad apologies or retractions of what had been spoken wrongly could have been avoided. He said.

We live in a country where a Governor or a Minster can apportion to himself all the Resources the State required to address it's problems and nothing ever happened to them. They get away with it. Do we talk about the Presidents that we have had and the one that we have now? He asked in anger. Why would I not do a simple task of assisting one Citizen that is the responsibility of the State to ship out of that State in search of a meaning in his life? He wondered in his rhetoric also directed at Omagbemi as well as anyone else who heard him.

Where Omagbemi requested for him to do something which could keep Abejide in America for six months or one year to make something meaningful with his life, Bolaji said he would see to it that Jide spent four or five years there at the expense of the State he had worked for to the best of his innate abilities for almost all his life time. He would engineer a Human Resource Development Programme of one year for Abejide within the next one month. Jide should work to get admission in any institution of learning there. That was easy to achieve there too. He said.

# CHAPTER SIX

# NO OUTLIVING THE WARMTH OF MOTHER

What did I tell you the very first time that you asked me, worrying, whether it would ever be possible for you to visit the States the night we went out in Brighton and ended up where we are today? Didn't I tell you that just as you did not know one year before that time, or in your own words even three days before we boarded the flight to London that you had no idea whatsoever that you could visit England, you would be in America without knowing yourself for that to happen, and that it is God who makes everything in the world possible? I told you. I remember that very well. In fact I remember telling you that much better than I remember what happened between us and later that same night that has landed us where we are today.

Bimbo was relieving her experience with Jide in England when his telephone call to her went through and he was proudly and very happily telling her about the miracle and grace of God in his life that were making his forth coming trip to the United States something even more unbelievable than a fairy tale to him.

He said he believed her when she told him that on that day that she was referring to just as he believed everything that she ever told him, including what she was telling him today.

Is it not because I believe you that I am on my way to meet you there? He asked her almost as if he was seeing her from where he was.

I believe you too. She said. I believe you too. There is no limit to what God can do in the life of any human being, especially those who have their trust, hopes and faith in Him. Those who totally believe in Him. She said she herself was in the favour of the same God they believed in.

She was in contact with her office in Will Rock and everything was pointing to her securing a study leave with pay for up to four years. That means that their twins would be born in the United States and win automatic Citizenship there. It would be up to the two of them when he arrived in Atlanta Georgia if they would return to their own country or decide to settle in the United states of America.

That is how awesome God is, Jide! Bimbo said. There is no situation beyond the control of God.

Motigbo! He told her, Motigbo meaning I have heard you – I have heard what you have said.

In less than three weeks from that day Jide would be touching down on American Soil at the John F Kennedy International Airport in New York City – New York City that had remained in his psyche only as a place in fairy land one month ago. And from there he would fly into Atlanta, Georgia to be received by his wife to be, the mother of his twins in the making and his brother in law to be as well!

He thought about his mother again as he reflected on the things which Bimbo had discussed with him in that very long telephone conversation in an equally long space – space maybe as long as the Earth was from the Moon – a distance as wide apart as between Ocean View City in Will Rock and Atlanta Georgia in the United States of America.

He thought about all the advices which she would give him. He thought about all the special food delicacies that she would be preparing for him to eat in the few weeks that he had left for him to stay with her here in Ocean View City, knowing fully well that soon he would be gone – gone far, far away from her. Gone to America land of limitless opportunities.

Most of all, Abejide missed the beautiful songs which his mother would be singing in praise of God The Creator of the Heavens and The Earth, for making it possible for her son Abejide to be heading towards the wonder of people around the world – the wonder of everyone on Earth, including people from England, the United Kingdom or Great Britain or whatsoever that place was called, which, Dei gracia, he had visited.

Mother, dear mother! He said in his mind as he picked his steps gradually back home where he knew that Madam Omagbemi the closest that anyone around this his space could be to his treasure of a mother was waiting to hear from him – waiting for him to tell her stories or news about how the people that he was going to meet Over The Sea there – Over The Sea which Will Rock Natives called people travelling outside the Shores of their lands, were preparing to receive him.

He felt empty inside him. If someone in your space is not the person that you would wish that they were, they cannot be that other person out of reach of you who you would wish that they were.

Abejide thought about what the people of the world said about wishes. Horses and beggars, would ride Horses if wishes were Horses, and then began to cry inside of him with a lot of pain – pain which he coud not explain even to he himself.

No. They cannot be. Omagbemi cannot be his mother, fantastic as she had been to him as an Aunty. That is what she is. And that is what she can be – the only thing that she can be to him to the end of time.

No one can be his mother or anything near her. It is not possible. He told himself as he walked along, his legs looking heavier than they were before he started the journey to the place he was coming from.

Mommy!
Mommy,
My dear
Mommy,
You are Oyinbo,
Yes!
There is
No doubt –
No doubt
Whatsoever
That you are
Oyinbo.

If I,
Abejide,
Your son,
Abejide,
Who, I am
Nobody –
Who, I am
Next to nobody,
Compared
To you,
I am
Packing myself
To go
To the land –
That beautiful land
Of the white man
Called Oyinbo,
Are you not
Yourself
Oyinbo?

Are you
Not there –
There before me?
There even before
My dream
To get there?

You are!
You are
Oyinbo,
Mommy!

Abejide heard himself talking to himself, not knowing whether the speech that he heard himself making inside of him was Song, Poetry or just a speech.

He tried to go back to the beginning of that Speech, Song or Poetry, but he found that he could not remember the order in which those string of words came to him at the time that came to him. He could not remember, and when he tried harder, could not remember as clearly as he felt that he should remember them. They came from inside of him, afterall. He told himself, angry and upset with himself still in his inside.

Why could he not remember what he heard inside of him just now? He wondered in great agony. Why would he not remember?

23

I just cannot remember. He told himself. Because I am not my mother. Yes, Jide, because you are not your mother! He heard himself say emphatically still inside of him. She could not have forgotten – she could not have forgotten even one word if she were the person who formed those words in her inside and brought them out the way that he did just now. She would never ever forget it.

What a shame. He told himself. What a shame. What a shame that two people could not be the same in every way even though they had the same blood or blood from the same source in them as between him and his mother as was the case staring him in his face where he was standing like a work of Art without a soul – without the breath of life inside of it.

What a shame. He told himself again as he walked along the lonely path to his abode where everyone who he was related to was, except the only person that he needed and wanted very badly to find in that vast space – his mother without whom everything was a void.

# CHAPTER SEVEN

# YOUR WILL ALL MUST OBEY, LORD

The Cake Designer, Carol Fitzgerald was invited to carry on with the Protocols leading up to the Cutting of the Cake.

There were the Zodiac Signs of Cupid with the Arrow, the Star and a pair of lovely Doves on the Huge Cake which Carol said symbolized the limitless nature of the human spirit and the stardom into which Jaiday and Bimbo oo oo had been admitted that day. She said.

At the count of the five letters of the name of Jesus called very loudly from the first letter J to the last letter S the cake was cut, with a Draw returned instantly as the Verdict handed down as the Result of the Keenly Fought Contest – a fight with neither injuries being inflicted nor blood being spilled.

The Bride fed the Bridegroom. The Bridegroom fed the Bride and the cake went round the Hall to every Guest in Attendance.

After all the worries, concerns, fears, frustrations, uncertainties, and last minute hype surrounding the long expected coming together of the two most recent visitors to the United States of America from Will Rock in Africa, South West of the Sahara Desert, the solemnization of Holy Matrimony between Abimbola Adedeji and Abejide Olanrewaji was complete and over with in a twinkle of an eye.

Abejide had spent a lot of time preparing for this moment. As a matter of fact, he started making notes and sketches of what he was going to say on this grand occasion of his life here far away from home even before he left the shores of Will Rock a forthright or so ago. He also made it known to the young woman sitting to his left hand side in the shining white apparel that he would want to be remembered by what he would say on that Wedding Reception occasion soon after the noise and razzmatazz of his historic arrival on American soil had died down. And she had agreed with him and encouraged him to continue to scribble bits and pieces of what he considered to be vital in that speech which he would not want to forget to include in it in the end.

Bimbo also apologized to him that she was not going to make any input to what he would say, most of which might also be directed at her or obvious references to her which would be best if those outpourings of strong emotions came to her as a surprise and not as what she had known well in advance, since traditionally, the woman – Bride that she would be called at that moment, would not, and should not have anything to say throughout the Ceremony.

She would very much love to hear her husband speak for the very first time since becoming her husband from deep in his heart which she had discovered to be very lovely a long time ago.

Demola Oloyode the Master of Ceremony was in his usual elements as he made the Announcement for the man who was responsible for everyone present in that Hall to be where they were by what he had planned to do before Independence and clinically executed after that Independence – Independence of whichever country, be it of the United States of America or of Will Rock, he did not say, to please open his heart to his first choice of a friend, a Partner, a Confidante and everything to him in his World.

Abejide was happy with the length of time that Demola Oloyode's Introduction lasted, as it afforded him the wonderful opportunity for him to go over the brief that he had made for himself as a guide to provide him with fodder for the canons that he would fire when he stood on his feet to talk to the crowd of people – a crowd of Distinguished people which included many fair skinned people – many Oyinbo people. And that was the first time that he was ever going to address a gathering of that mixture of colours and of Races – that Rainbow of Races, yes. He had told himself very clearly.

As a result he had paid so much attention to looking over those notes that he had made for himself for quick reference, and, consequently, did not listen to the Talk Master Demola Oloyode talking about him so much that when he was called upon to take to the stand to make the speech, he did not hear the bell ring just as a punch drunk Boxer would not hear the bell at the start of the next round and be counted out.

It was the prompting of the woman about whom and because of whom he was where he was both in that country and in that one tiny space of massive Uncle Sam that roused him to the understanding of time beckoning on him and to action, yes – time beckoning on him even to the action of his rising to his feet as well as to the occasion – the making of the speech which he had prepared for to make for nearly his entire life time.

He rose to his feet and to the occasion in the end, and at the end of it all did not disappoint himself or his best half Bimbo or anyone else there for that matter. He gave himself Pass Marks as did his wife Bimbo.

I will like to first and foremost, give gratitude to *Olodumare* – God The Almighty, Father of the whole World and the entire Universe for making it possible for what I am experiencing with my two eyes and with my full consciousness to be happening here that I am with all the people present here too. He said and then knelt down, raising his two hands to the high Heavens above.

Bimbo signalled to Oprah her Chief Brides Maid to give her a helping hand for her to also kneel down.

Oprah obliged her and also knelt down with her behind her – Oprah the girlfriend of her brother Olufemi Adedeji who was as thrilled in what she was experiencing as the woman for whom she was like an alter ego – like a Siamese twin baby – Bimbo the Bride whose every bidding she must do until the day was over.

Marcello the Cuban American friend of Olufemi's who was playing the role of Best Man did not kneel down beside or behind the man he had agreed to be Batman for today. He stood like a Soldier at a Forte – a Sentry, and only watched over the three people closest to him in his space keenly but silently.

I shall ask for forgiveness from the crowd of the wonderful people here – forgiveness from God Almighty, and for their patience with me too, and for their understanding, should any one of them feel that I am taking too much time praising you, adoring you, and magnifying you, Father of Mankind, for all your wondrous works in my life. Please bear with me, people of God! And join me to praise Him! Join me to magnify Him! Join me to sing Hallelujah! Hosanna in the Highest to His Mighty name! Who would have thought one year ago, that I, Abejide Olanrewaju, that I could be on these hallowed grounds called America, The United States of America! And being married to this Angel of a woman – Bimbo beside me today, being joined in holy matrimony to me by no less a Personage than the proud American Priest Kelly Reuben, if it is not the Lord's doing? May Your Mighty name be forever praised! Forever be magnified and Adored! Jehovah Jireh! Lord Emmanuel here with me and everywhere! The I Am That I Am! And may you continue to bless the soul of my mother Lola, as she sits near you as close as anyone can be to perfection even as you blessed her while she sojourned here. If not for your Will which all must obey, Lord, who would make it impossible for her to be here in this glittering Hall today to sing your praise? Thank you, mommy! Thank you, mommy Lola for bringing me into the world to carry your photograph with me wherever I go. Thank you, Lord God Almighty for your grace. Thank you, Lord, for Bimbo who you gave to me. Thank you, Lord, for the multiple Gifts which you have given to us already! Thank you, Lord, for the life of my brother Femi and all Members of his families in Will Rock and all over the world. Thank you, Lord, for the Priest that joined us! Thank you for all of your Hand Maidens here who witnessed the solemnization of the Wedding that has entered the Guinness Book of my life. I ask you, God Almighty, to please take total and absolute control of my life, the life of Bimbo my sweet and lovely wife, and guide our footpaths, direct our every course that we walk and protect us under your mighty Wings, that we should not and do not falter in our commitment, faithfulness and truthfulness to each other, neither come to any harm nor want from this day even unto the end of our time here on Earth, according, and, only according to Your Will! Amen! Amen, Lord! And all these I have asked from you in the name of the Father! Amen. In the name of the Son! Amen. And in the name of the Holy Spirit! Amen!

Amen! The crowd responded on all three counts and broke into a hilarious and riotous clapping, banter and frenetic gyration. And then the Bridal Dance followed!

The Band did a very popular marriage Party Song, and ended with For He is a Jolly Good Fellow which threw the Hall into a wild bout of drunken dancing and gyrating.

Distinguished Ladies and Gentlemen! The Master of Ceremony said. You will all agree with me, I bet, that that was one hell of a speech or an Address of The Bride Groom that we have heard at a Wedding Reception. Congratulations, Mister and Misses Olarewanju! And may your road be smooth all the way through!

One hour, thereafter, the Massive Romeo Palace, Venue of the Marriage Reception was empty almost as though nothing happened there, not only today or a few moments ago, but since the birth of the world.

At home in their own Apartment, everything was low keyed in consideration of the condition that Bimbo the Iyawo Tuntun – Iyawo Tuntun meaning in Yoruba the Brand New Wife was in.

Honey Moon? Yes, and No. Where they were, was it not the equivalent of the Moon itself, coming from as far as they did come?

Honey? The sweetness or bitterness of any fruit was only a factor of the condition of the tongue that tasted it.

Bimbo and Jide had tasted honey way back in England many moons ago – honey that tasted just as sweet, thereafter, and was even getting progressively sweeter by the day.

Five years rolled by like the twinkle of stars at night that faded with the sudden appearance of daylight from nowhere.

Little Bimbo and Jide were already doing very well in the Kinder Garten School located within five minutes walk from where the older Bimbo and Jide lived, all of them happy with the new environment that was far from Femi's Apartment in Atlanta, Georgia.

Jide and Bimbo had obtained two University Degrees each – a Baccalaureate and a Masters Degree – Jide in Public Administration and Bimbo in Banking and Finance.

Jide was moving further in his quest to become a Doctor, not of the human Anatomy or of the Soul of man, but a Doctor of the human Mind – of the human mind – yes, to become the Holder of a Doctor of Philosophy Degree.

He clocked in and clocked out of the Museum of African Art Offices where he was Assistant Curator while he attended his compulsory Lectures in aid of his Doctorate twice every week and to discuss his Dissertation with the Maverick Professor Thompson Reeves of the State University of Baltimore, Maryland.

Can you please defend your claim that Ignorance and not the Criminal Desire or Propensity to Defraud The Nation is responsible for the Underdevelopment And Impoverishment of Third World Countries, Will Rock as your Case Study, Professor Spike Kaiser, Chairman of The Panel examining the Content of his Dissertation asked Jide Olanrewaju as he sat in front of the Seven Man Team of Investigators to the suitability or otherwise of one more Candidate for Admission to the Exclusive Intellectual Club of Philosophers styled as Doctor in all parts of the world except France where only Medical Doctors were acknowledged that way, while everyone else was a Mister, but where every Teacher or Lecturer was addressed as Professor whereas in every other country of the world, Teachers and Lecturers moved from lower levels of their teaching Professions to become Readers and ultimately Professors.

Thank you my dear Professor – Jide Olanrewaju started but was quickly halted. It was the same Professor Spike Kaiser who had asked him the question who now spoke to interrupt him.

Sorry. Cut all your niceties! No embellishments. No greetings. Go straight to the substance of what I have asked you. He said.

Ignorance. Jide Olanrewaju picked off from there without any more ado. Is the greatest malaise anywhere mankind is in existence. Ignorance, yes, ignorance, more than anything else. And it is for a simple reason, which is, that it has no cure and will never have a cure except for the cure that the sufferer himself will provide to himself or to themselves, not through any known medicines or therapies, but by shaking off the ignorance – by shaking off the disease itself by becoming aware of the self, by becoming aware of the evil that they did not know before. By becoming aware that only the search for knowledge of the damage which their not knowing the cause and the effect of what they are doing can change them, and, changing them, also change Society itself, and can alter the situation!

Stop! Professor Spike Kaiser said. Do we have other questions for our Candidate here? He asked the six other Professors, all of them wearing long and white beards except the man who had spoken to them.

Nope. The six other Professors said one after the other.

Very well then. Professor Spike Kaiser said. We shall break for Lunch for one hour. You may go for lunch yourself, Jaide. Or take a walk – just take a walk. But please be sure to be back here fifty minutes from now – not one second later. It's past Eleven O'Clock now. So we expect to see you back here precisely at noon. Enjoy yourself. Professor Spike Kaiser said as he walked away from Abejide.

Abejide did not know what to say at that point. He was afraid to say Thank you or anything like that.

Professor Spike Kaiser may view that as another unnecessary embellishment or distraction, or maybe an attempt on his part to bribe the Panel?

He stood up from the lonely desk where he had sat for the past nearly one hour and began to make his way to the door leading out of the Architectural beauty of the Faculty Board Room.

He placed a call to Bimbo his wife once he was outside the Hall.

The eggheads have gone off for Lunch Break. He told her, sounding very low and cold.

How long have they engaged you before that break? She asked him.

Effectively, less than half an hour. He told her. Less than one hour. He repeated for clarity and emphasis.

What did they tell you last before you left the Viva Hall? She asked him, sounding worried from her tone of voice.

O I remember that very well. He told her. The man said Enjoy yourself!

Ah! Jaid! He said so? Bimbo asked him, sounding upbeat all of a sudden.

Yes, Bimo oo. That's what he told me. He said I should enjoy myself, but make sure that I was back there in the Hall not one second later than noon. I wonder in what way he wants me to enjoy myself, my dear wife.

*Opari*! Bimbo said, jubilating, *Opari* meaning in Yoruba It is finished! It means, Honey, that you have made it! Congratulations! She added, sounding very happy and excited.

Is that so? Jide asked her in great surprise. How did you know this? He asked her.

Yes, darling! Bimbo screamed. I ran into an old friend of mine here – an old girl friend whose brother went through what you are going through there now, not long ago. He says that it is their euphemism of letting you know without telling you in plain language that you have made it! And, of course, I will believe it. I will believe what he told me for two reasons. One. Why would you, my dear husband that I know the way that I know you, fail in any examination? No way! That is not possible! Two. Why would that Professor ask anyone who they were still examining, to go and enjoy themselves, if he knew that the person might not make it? That too is not possible. Therefore, Congratulations, my dear AB! She said, laughing hilariously.

# CHAPTER EIGHT

## EXCLUSIVE CLUB OF DOCTORS OF PHILOSOPHY

Thank you, Bim-Bim. Abejide said, not quite sure of the emotions that his voice signalled. I have to go back now. It is almost getting to noon on the dot. He said as the telephone conversation between him and Bimbo his wife came to an abrupt end.

Good to see you back, Abejayeeday! Professor Spike Kaiser told him after everyone was back in their chairs.

Abejide did not say anything. He listened for what next and for what else he would be told.

We are about to break with our age old tradition here, Sir. Professor Spike Kaiser said, looking Abejide straight in his eyes. Usually, our Doctoral Candidates would go through their entire Dissertation and take questions from all Members of the Assessment Team, and then leave, to wait to hear from the President of the Faculty in days, and, sometimes for a few months after the Oral Defense. In your own case, however, we have reached a decision to address you as Doctor Abejaiday Olanirewajuu! Is that right? Olanizewajuu? He stopped to ask the Candidate the correct pronunciation of his name Olanrewaju.

Abejide kept mum. He did not want to be the spoil sport himself. He did not want to be cut short by anyone in the same Hall twice on the same day.

You do not believe me. Professor Spike Kaiser said. Or do you? He asked Abejide.

I don't quite understand. Abejide said.

I understand perfectly. Professor Spike Kaiser said. I will like you to be upstanding, Sir, as we come round to admit you to our proud fold and Exclusive Club of Philosophy Doctors, and say Congratulations to you!

Abejide got up as though he were electric operated, his two hands by his sides.

Well done for your fine job in dealing with your subject.

Professor Olegrad Woodrow told him.

Pretty good job that you did. Professor Donald Woodstone told him.

One more thing. Professor Spike Kaiser said as everyone stood in their space. We've secured an Offer of Appointment for you in the upgraded Institute of Africa American Studies as a Senior Lecturer if you will accept the Offer. That's number one. Number two. Whether you are able to accept the Offer or not, we also have a Speaking Opportunity for you at our Conference on The Future of Afrocentricism. That is going to happen in the next three weeks. You should look through your excellent Dissertation and come up with an appropriate Presentation which you can further develop as a different Project from the Doctoral Thesis that it is at the moment, to also Publish it as a book.

Do you know how much that Speaking Platform is giving you? Professor Kaiser asked Abejide who was still mum and in something like dream land. He had not come to terms with what he had heard so far. He had to say something, anyway, because Professor Spike Kaiser was not saying anything else. He was just looking at Abejide just as all his other Colleagues were doing in the frozen silence.

My dear Professor, Sir. Abejide said. Please allow me, first of all, to thank you for Congratulating me on my scaling through the Pee Hetch Dee Hurdle. I do hope I am right to think so? If I am, I really do appreciate it. Let me also thank you for the Employment that you say is mine for the taking not even for the asking. Isn't that wonderful? It is! And because it is coming from this place which I now see as home to me, I will very seriously consider taking it when I look at what is there in the package for me. Finally, Sir, let me also jump at the Speaking Opportunity that you have also secured for me. It will be my very first chance of testing the veracity of my conclusions and arguments in my Thesis. That will be most wonderful! Then let me ask you this question – How much is that giving me as you said? I mean the Speech that I should be giving?

Professor Spike Kaiser looked at Abejide with a lot of interest and admiration. He went close to his left ear and whispered to the awe struck Abejide You gonna be making Five Grand for an hour long Speech, and maybe a few questions as follow up. Less than, or not more than two hours. Good, isn't it? He asked him.

Pretty good! Abejide said.

The Seven Professors led Abejide into the Restaurant attached to the Faculty of Management Engineering Sciences, and soon, they were eating an early Dinner – their long standing tradition for Scholars who successfully defended their Doctoral Theses being put on full display.

Bimbo was exceedingly pleased and proud of her husband after he broke the entire News Calabash to her.

Abejide should accept the Teaching Appointment. She would accompany him to the Five Thousand Dollar Presentation Event in the next three weeks where he would be introduced for the very first in his life as Doctor Abejide Olanrewaju.

What can God not do in the life of those who laid their trust and all their hopes and expectations on Him? They asked in awe of The Great Architect of The Entire Universe.

# CHAPTER NINE

## LADY OMAGBEMI ARRIVES IN MARYLAND TO HONOUR DOCTOR ABEJIDE

At long last Lady Omagbemi was being expected to arrive in the United States of America to visit Abejide her Nephew and his wife Bimbo who no one could describe as a new wife anymore. No. Not after their lovely set of twins had been born, and after they had spent two long years together there.

Abejide had wanted very badly for her to attend their Wedding Ceremony nearly six years ago. Yes, he wanted very badly for her to be there as the closest he could get to his own mother being there herself at that threshold of the history of his chequered life. Yes, the history that he was making in far away America.

But Lady Omagbemi had been very forthright in telling him that it was too early for her to visit. And that was how it stayed. Abejide reflected on her reasons for doing what she did long after the Marriage had been solemnized.

One. She counted. He had not fully acclimatized in the new country and it's new challenges that he was facing. Two. All of them were staying with Bimbo's older brother Olufemi Adedeji. The Apartment meant for one family would be too compact to give each and every one of them the freedom and the appropriate space required for them to be as free as they would like or want to be and to enjoy themselves. Yes, enjoy themselves, why not? Enjoyment was a veritable part of life and living – a great part of travelling and the Yoruba people's way of life which they called Ilabe e.

When they were to be awarded their Masters' Degrees, they had also extended an invitation to her, but there too Lady Omagbemi gave three reasons as to why she could not make the trip she was being begged to make – three reasons all of which Abejide told his wife were but lame excuses – excuses which, he said, she gave only in order for her not to visit. And she did not come too. She did not show up in the end.

Now, with Abejide harnessing the big one called the Doctorate which would be Awarded to him one week before he would occupy centre stage as the Speaker on the Special Area of his Ph.D Thesis, she felt obliged to visit. She could no longer find any justification to be absent.

She was accordingly met on arrival at the Baltimore Airport by seven persons.

There were her Chief Hosts to be – Abejide and his wife Bimbo – Bimbo or Abimbola who was harbouring a secret which no one knew yet but one person apart from she herself.

There was Olufemi Adedeji who had made their initial stay in the magic country called America or Uncle Sam very comfortable and enjoyable – Olufemi Adedeji or Femi, Bimbo's older brother.

The under seven Players – Bejide and Bimbola Junior were also there in their own right as Members of The Will Rock Eleven Football Squad in The Diaspora.

There was Oprah the Chief Brides Maid at the Ceremony of a little over five years ago whose grouse with Femi Adedeji was increasing by the day as a result of what both of them knew and could see with their unclothed eyes – Bimbo and Abejide who were now man and wife and no longer the boyfriend and girlfriend that they were on their separate arrivals there.

Demola Oloyode was there too.

And so, Technically speaking, the Matriarch Omagbemi was actually being received by eight people, the last of whom could not be seen yet but was there.

She arrived with little Sola of five years ago who was now five years older, and, therefore, was also no longer as little as he was five years ago.

Lady Omagbemi complained well ahead of the very crowded Reception Programme which the seven or eight persons had arranged for her on her arrival – a Programme, which, after they unfolded it to her with the kind of happiness and spirit of out doing each other to execute, forced tears of joy from her tired eyes.

I am not as young as any one of you here is anymore. She said when they ran through what had been lined up for her on that day of her arrival. I am also no longer as young and as vibrant as Jide would think that I used to be as he saw me to be before he left home. Therefore, my dear lovely children, I will like to take everything very easy. Easy, indeed – very easy, very much aware that there will also be a tomorrow ahead of us no matter how many things we did or accomplished today. There will always be a tomorrow in front of us which we will never catch up with but meet after it has left – after it has gone away from where it was in the tomorrow that we saw yesterday, and which we can only meet as today, not that tomorrow that it will continue to be to us whenever we get there permanently.

Notwithstanding her plea for them to cut down on the activities which they had lined up for her even before she got over her jet lag, though, Lady Omagbemi was the person who requested that they should please spend a little more time than they apportioned for to spend at the live Performance of two African American Hip Hop Artistes they went to see Perform at the Mohammed Ali Arcade.

Back home to the Olanrewaju's Apartment, like Abejide, when he returned from his first ever trip Abroad to England with his endless stories about how NEPA never went away where he had just come from, she never stopped talking about the beauty of the Performance of the Blind Opheus as she called the Artiste who had been blind from the day that he was born, and the African American Lady of Songs who everyone acknowledged as such.

Thank you, Omo mi. She kept telling everyone, including Demola Oloyede, Omo mi meaning My Children in Yoruba.

She did not give any space to Demola Oloyode for him to protest her including him as one of her children. He held his fire too, telling himself that there would be time someday somewhere and somehow for him to speak his mind to her on that her wrong classification or taxonomy of his also being her child. That time never came. It was just as well because Lady Omagbemi never gave a thought to it and would have been greatly surprised if she heard him complain.

What was there in it to complain? She would wonder and move on after saying ma binu – or don't be angry.

The twins became permanently gummned to Lady Omagbemi, following her everywhere, even into the wash room whenever she had need to go there.

What a pair of lovely children! She would think to herself. Ha! Ha! What an impossible pair of scissors!

Ah! She would scream with boundless joy. You will love me to death oo oo oo, you these my great grand children!

And then she would laugh by her fascination by their own innocent laughters, not associating anything wrong or over the board with what they were doing in following her into the only place where no one else accompanied any one else.

They were only acting their age, afterall. And one day that ignorance – that ignorance would be gone and gone forever. She told herself each and every time that they invaded her privacy the way that they did in their naked innocence.

The long Greyhounds Bus ride from Baltimore to Atlanta was the second most pleasant event for Lady Omagbemi and Sola – particularly for Sola who stayed glued to the window of the long snake, taking in the beautiful scenery as the big eared Dog sped by.

Auntie! He called Lady Omagbemi, full of energy and excitement.

Hello, dear! She answered him, exposing her pair of red rose lips that always thrilled the only man who came around to visit her or to take her out for very long hours way back home in Ocean View City in Will Rock. These Buses are better than our Buses in Ocean View City. Sola said, frowning as he said so. He was angry at what he was seeing far away from home which was in very sharp and painful contrast to what he knew to be the ugly truth in his own Land. Why was it so? He asked her.

My dear! Lady Omagbemi said. You have to tell me one thing that you will see here from now until we go back home, which is not better than what we have at home. Just one thing that you can point to me or to any one else here as something that is not as good as what we have at home or is even worse than what we have there. Then I will answer you or agree or disagree with you in what you have observed. She said, smiling sleepily as the Bus tore away. Try. Try very hard as we go from place to place and from day to day if you can show me just one thing that is not better than what we have back at home before we leave, and I will record it in indelible ink in my Diary and inside the Diary where you don't need ink to record anything. Do you get me, Sho-Sho oo oo? She asked Sola who clasped his two hands as if to suggest that it would not be long before he proved her wrong. And so he looked at everything that he saw in a very strange way, hoping to unravel something in it which would make his dream of contradicting Lady Oma come true.

If that is what you have decided to concentrate to find, then you better relax, Sola. She told him soon. You have to relax because it will be something which will take very long if not forever for you to find. She told him when she discovered how desperate and anxious he was to find what would be worse off here than there back home in Will Rock as an agenda that he must execute.

Auntie! Sola whispered very loudly into Lady Omagbemi's right ear on the Grounds of the Six Flags Amusement Park.

Yes, dear! She answered as usual, not knowing what she was going to hear him say this time in this Dream World that was real.

I don't want to go back with you when you want to go, Auntie. He said. I know, Sho oo oooo oo. I know. She said. And she did not go any further to say anything else. She let it be as he had said it and as she had answered it too – as tersely and as off handedly as she had done.

Sola saw that as an approval of his request for him to stay back in the United States when it would be time for her to leave for home, until she told him one day when he was not expecting to hear what she told him matter of factly, that he should please use the experience that he was having here in the United States of America of his dreams as ingredient to wet his appetite to read his books more vigorously than he did before so that he could pass all his exams very well and win a Scholarship back home to return here to study and later to also come back here to work like Jide, like Bimbo and like Femi, but should set his eyes on returning home with her on this his maiden trip by and by. Their return together was non negotiable. She told him.

# CHAPTER TEN

# NO MORE A JJC

When our Resource Person returned to Ocean View City where he had lived all his life on his first ever Overseas trip to England nearly seven years ago, the woman who he married here in The United States at a very colourful Ceremony about six years or so ago, was the first person to call him by the sobriquet or acronym JJC or Johnny Just Come that nearly got stuck on him as his pseudonym to the point of replacing his actual names that strangely were also very close to that acronym Jide or Abejide Alanrewaju.

Shedding the bark or the slough of the New Comer very quickly, he faced what brought him here in the first place squarely and obtained a Masters Degree in Public Administration three years or so ago with a Distinction in all vital Areas of his Study.

He carried that Torch of Distinction to the next Frontier of his avid Search for Knowledge and for Excellence – in his Doctoral Enquiry where his Faculty Board had to re-write their long standing tradition and rules to Announce his scaling every hurdle to him at a Session which was designed to grill him to his bones for him to prove his worth and to satisfy his tried and tested Examiners that he was, indeed, the man who wrote the Thesis that they all had in front of them.

The Faculty got a Job for him as a Senior Lecturer even before he appeared in person to defend his Thesis.

And it was as a result of the waves which his Ground Breaking Research work was making that he landed the Position of his being The Choice of The Speaker at today's epochal Event.

Royce Angelo the Italian American University Orator who was functioning as Master of Ceremony of the Event went on and on talking about the Excellence which had become the Hallmark of Abejide Olanrewaju's character and integrity on the Academic Frontier so much that the Audience of Distinguished Academics, Industrialists and Politicians were tired of applauding the man being talked about as he stood in the middle of the Quincy Adams Events Centre in the Spotlight, his brown Yoruba Agbada with the cap called Aja – meaning Dog's ear, exuding confidence, modesty and great satisfaction with a tinge of inescapable pride or hubris. More pride than hubris. Or maybe just pride. Hubris? No. It was not in his nature to behave with that kind of levity.

His Doctorate, Awarded to him at a Record Breaking Time, Place and Ceremony, is hardly two weeks old, but our man of the moment, Doctor Abejide Olanrewaju, is such a Phenomenal Speaker and Committed Activist when it comes to his views about Race Relations and the Politics that fuels it that I am left in no doubt that we are in for as much delight as we are in for surprise. That we are in for as much sleep as we are in for an awakening and a re-awakening in a lot of thoughts that we here have hung on to before today as what we believe in and as what we are ready to stand for and to die for, no matter the odds that we face.

Let me not reveal everything but leave some for you to find out for yourselves – through your own discoveries as I invite and present to you our Speaker today On Race Relations, Africa American Ethnocentrisms And The Politics Of Colour And Performance, Doctor Abejide Olanrewaju as he does the kick off! Pee Eitch Dee, Senior Lecturer, Institute of Afro American Studies, State University of Maryland, Baltimore! Doctor Abejide Olanrewaju, please!

Doctor Abejide Olanrewaju bowed to the Four Cardinal Points of the well lit Hall and walked up to the Podium, his Speech inside the file which he held in his right hand.

He stopped now again to acknowledge the riotous cheers. And the more he stopped to bow the louder the ovation roared.

The Audience clapped once more and gave him a standing ovation after he got to the Podium. What an Introduction! What a Morning! The Members of the Audience said one to the other.

While the standing ovation lasted, Dr. Abejide Olanrewaju took the opportunity to talk to God who he was well aware was The Only Force responsible for his being at the Podium upon which he was standing at that time as He was and Has been for everything that had happened in his life.

Thank you, Olodumare.

Thank you, Olonwun Oba.

Thank you, Lord God Almighty!

He said, ending the prayer in which he did nothing but praise and Thank God The Creator of the Entire Universe.

I wish I can say Fellow Americans!

I wish I can say Fellow Citizens of The United States!

I wish I can call for a Tea and Coffee Break even before we have started, for us to allow for time – time, that phenomenon that is like no other phenomenon in the whole wide world – time which shapes our every action, time which guides our every path, no matter the journey that we go on, time which scores us as we pass or fail without making excuses or showing emotions – time which no one ignores without dire consequences, time which everyone knows is there and rules their lives, and yet which those who have no one else to blame but they themselves do not know is there in sufficient quantity for them to do anything and everything that they are expected to do when they fail to do those things – time, the only thing that is unstoppable even when we can see the tiny hand that counts the little seconds away that lead to minutes and to long hours, many days, several weeks, multiple months, years, decades, Centuries, Millennia and more, and yet does not falter where all else falters – time which no one can stop, be it analogue or quartz or Digital time as in the physical time that we see! For, if you can break the hands of the ancient clock, if you can take out the batteries or unplug the cable linking the modern day Digital Clock from the socket to say or claim that you have stopped it, what about the time that ticks on even at that moment of your madness on the Ocean Tops and Great River beds? On the Skies beyond the Clouds where Rotation and Revolution go on unimpeded? What about the time under the left side of your chest that ticks on in the parts of your body which we call the heart, which, if it stops beating to declare you dead, does not stop time which will, instead, record when you died? Where you died? And how you ceased to be? How that came to be?

Time sees the very best of mankind and womankind being born in it's presence, and sees the greatest, the wealthiest, the most famous, the most accomplished and the most powerful and influential men and women of the world also die in it's presence, as well as provides the only balm that heals the wounds, that tempers the pains and the sadness occasioned by those deaths with itself by it's mere passage – Time's passage which brings those calamities to the deep past where memory begins to fade and makes the erstwhile tortured minds begin to forget, and in amnesia, makes the assailed come to terms with the pains, the frustrations, the sadness, the helplessness and the hopelessness of the gulf and the stark reality of the void created by the loss also through Time's own passage. Time, O time! Are you not God Himself Who we see with our unclothed eyes but still do not know? Is that not what you are, Time?

That is what my mind tells me that you are, Time, old Time! That is what I think that you are! Yes! Time – Time before anything came to be – Time with everything that there is and everything that there are anywhere and everywhere even beyond the Universe – Time that endures after everything else is gone … and remains what it is – Unchanging and unchangeable … Time that eats no food … Time that has multiple eyes and sees everything but does not see anything … Time that has uncountable ears and hears everything spoken as well as unspoken and yet does not hear anything … Time that does not grow old and never ever dies …

Doctor Abejide Olanrewaju spoke on like the possessed Maverick that he had suddenly become, not paying any attention to what his Listeners did or did not do. He spoke on and on, gesturing where he must and observing silence where he must too. He was a beauty of a big Masquerade to behold. An nnukwu nmmawuu the Ibos would say, or Owu Alagba or the Masquerade after whose performance no other Masquerade ever performs – the Show Stopper, the Kalabari would say.

# CHAPTER ELEVEN

# TIME, ARE YOU NOT THE SAME AS GOD?

The Listeners were all on their feet, and had stopped clapping. They had stopped clapping, not because there was nothing more for them to cheer. They were not clapping anymore, not because their palms now pained them. No. Not because they were tired of clapping. No. They had stopped clapping because that was the only thing that they could do in the circumstance – to show and to tell themselves, that not clapping was their way of clapping permanently and non-stop. Yes. To show that every word that issued forth from the mouth of the man who they had come to hear speak was gold and diamond worth the simple action of clapping non-stop for and standing up for forever.

They had been completely arrested and mesmerized by what he was saying even in his greetings to them or his introductory statements, every word of which was going deep into their Diaries – Diaries seen in the forms of recording equipment like telephone recorders or television Cameras, but unseen Diaries which every person's brain represented. The man who was affecting their behaviour that way was not aware of what they were doing or the turmoil that they were going through. If he was aware of it he did not care about how they felt or about how they behaved. He did not show any sign that he saw it or that he knew anything about it.

He cared only about the path which the Lord God his Creator had charted for him to go.

I will like to posit this thought which I have kept to myself for very long, that we should all come to agreement that Time is God and that God is Time – that He loves us so much that if He allowed us to see Him with our physical eyes we would not let him have one second of rest, but He gave us the nearest thing that can represent Him for us to see and to appreciate Him without touching Him and without altering His Will in the Instrument that we call Time. I shall hold you to that Agreement at the end of my Presentation if you will agree with me! I shall hold each and every one of us here to agree on that position of mine before this speaking Event is over. Please think about it. Give it a thought. Give it a thought no matter your religion, no matter your Faith!

I wish I can declare myself a bona fide Citizen of The State of Maryland in this country – Maryland which combines the name of the mother of Jesus and Land which everyone lays claims to, which, like The Virgin Mary herself and Land everywhere in the world have been good to me! Very good to me, indeed.

I wish I can call the man who spoke first here in order that he might introduce me to you, Gentleman Royce Angelo my brother! Yes. I wish I can call him my brother. Yes.

My brother, so that whatsoever I decide to say about what he has been extremely generous and gracious enough to say about me, he will know that it is coming from a brother and not from an enemy even though he construes it to be friendly fire or from an enemy who is a friend and a brother all in one!

Thank you, my brother, for situating me the way that you have done. Thank you for the grace with which you did it to assure me and all your hearers that it came straight from your heart raw and uncensored, and not because you are being paid to do so.

Whenever any person is honest, every other honest heart also sees it and feels it as it is, just as they see and feel when a person has been dishonest in what he claims to say honestly.

That is the truth about life that I know very well! That is the truth that I know.

Thank you for letting me know that I am no longer green in my ways here in Uncle Sam and of the ways of the world! Thank you for letting me know that I am yellow, amber and about to become red, and, therefore, that I am also about to hear the moment in which, like everyone else, someday, somehow, I will fall off the cliff!

Thank you for letting me know that I am no longer a Johnny who has Just Come or a Jay-Jay-Cee! JJC!

And now, please permit me to go back in time to reflect on what someone who knows better than me said long, long ago.

Do you remember the Magician of words – his words, especially when they are spoken in his Drama – on the Stage of the world he placed them which he says is everywhere in the world when he says I can well be moved if I were as you? I am talking about Julius Caesar speaking himself as he was asked to speak by his Creator the inimitable William Shakespeare in the book of that name and Protagonist – Julius Caesar in Julius Caesar!

I will refuse to humour myself to be moved by all the wonderful things that you said about me, brother Royce Angelo, which, instead of gingering me to action, have frightened me and warned me to be very careful.

So, because if we are wise and sensible enough to learn from that declaration by Julius Caesar in Julius Caesar, we will know that whenever men and women begin to praise you the most, that is the time for you to look out for the dagger hidden long ago being pointed at you right behind you where you stand, by your closest friend called Brutus or by any other name that you may know him to bear, even though you are not seeing him yet!

I will not be moved enough to be swollen headed by what I have been said to be, because I know my modest, my obscure and rustic origins, and the path that I have walked to get here for only God The Almighty knows how long.

When I look at the time that we all can see on the walls of this Hall, I can see that we have transitted from morning to afternoon already. Suppose I had said Good Morning a few moments ago?

Suppose, just for the purpose of argument, that I had said Good Morning twenty minutes ago, would we not be tempted to say that this Event happened in the Morning? In the Morning, no matter in what Poetic manner we describe that morning either as Cloudless, Sun lit, Bright or Rosy?

What do we do about the point that time has led us to now?

Would we also say that the Event happened in the Afternoon?

What if we are here until we have to say Good Evening before the Programme is over – Good Evening as some people somewhere are saying already by the Planetary Arrangement of The Great Architect of The Universe?

Is it not all a factor of the irreversibility of Time that I talked about? Time that is, Time that was, and Time that will continue to be? No matter who dies and no matter who is born or whatsoever happened howsoever and wherever?

Let us reflect on that. Let us give a thought to that.

I have brought with me here, fifty slides which we shall show to you on the television monitors all around us – slides for me to show you in graphic language what I have here in what we call hard copy soft as it is, as the Speech that I have been invited to deliver to you here, and, through you, to the whole wide world.

Please bear with me as we go into the heart of the matter that we are gathered here for to discuss.

Afro American Culture, Traditions, Behaviours. Afrocentrcism! Race Relations! That is the broad outline of my Speech.

What are we talking about in those taxonomies or classifications?

Look all around you and also look all about you and ask yourself Does anyone else that you see as you look round and about, look exactly the way that you yourself look – exactly the same way as you are in colour and Architectural Engineering Design Configuration?

From your hairs to your palms, even when the person sitting next to you is your brother or your sister born of the same biological mother and of the same biological father?

Even when you know very well that you were told that you had to be separated at birth as Siamese Twins? That the person sitting next to you is your sister or your brother?

Look in front of you and then look further ahead of you. Do the pictures or the images of the people that you see in front of you approximate the images of those people who are farther away from you?

Don't the people look progressively smaller in size the farther away from you, you look?

And while that is the truth, is it not also the truth that those who are farther away from you that look smaller are as small as they look to you or that they are as big as they are where they are to those sitting close to them – as big as they will be if anyone sitting farther away from you should change their sitting position and come and sit next to you while the person who has changed positions with that person goes to sit where that person stood up from to come and sit next to you?

What does this tell us?

What does that tell us but that we are all one and the same people, no matter where we are? That we are only as big as or as small as we are, no matter our distances from each other?

That we are all one and the same people no matter how much we may think, act and argue to the contrary?

That is the truth – the gospel truth as we say.

We are nothing else but Members of one Humanity – The same Humanity!

# CHAPTER TWELVE

# UNCLE SAM IGNORANT ONLY BY CHOICE

Let us see what we have on slide one. Thank you. Please bear with me. I will not take too much of your time.

No. I will not. And I should not because Time is precious, and is the only Asset which once gone, is gone forever, and which we all need to do whatsoever we have to do.

What you see there is a complete void somewhere in this Earth Reality that we know.

I will tell you where it is at the end of my Presentation.

Let us move quickly to slide number two – yes, slide two and rapidly move from there to slides three up to slide ten.

They show a transformation from the void that we saw in the first slide to what we are seeing in slide ten, to tell us the story and the truth of man's ingenuity which is in fulfillment of the Declaration of The Great Architect and Creator of The Entire Universe in the Book of Genesis that man should have Dominion Over Everything else that He Created and brought into being.

Slide Eleven is showing us turmoil – turmoil which is dragging us back to slides ten to slide one, instead of moving us forward to what we should expect to find from slides twelve to the slides ahead of twenty!

I will go on to show you from the Lap Top that I have in front of me, a Kaleidoscope of images that we see around our world today which we brand as Civilized in a broad generic term.

Or the world which we have classified into Three Broad Outlines as First World, Second World and Third World Countries.

Or are the First Two not First and Second World Countries?

If they are not, why do we agree that the Third should be labeled as Third World Countries?

The summation of my interpretation of what we have is that the behaviour of the people in what we call Third World countries derived from the behaviours of those people in what we call First and Second World Countries who themselves started from positions worse than what we find in today's Third, Fourth and Fifth World Countries which abound even though we are too ashamed to admit it to ourselves – that they are there the way that they are.

I remember Professor Spike Kaiser asking me on the day I felt more frightened about my abilities and shortcomings more than on any other day what, in my own opinion, is responsible for the Underdevelopment And Impoverishment of Third World Countries, with my Country, Will Rock As Case Study!

At that same time, somebody screamed as loudly as he could in one corner of the Auditorium saying That's the man I've come to hear speak!

Everyone turned their heads to see who that person shouting like a mad man could be.

Doctor Abejide Olanrewaju stopped his speech too to also look in the same direction where the noise was coming from.

He saw who it was and he was immediately overcome with emotion.

He fought tears which were forming rapidly in the well of his two eyes. He was fighting very hard to stop them from spilling over to wet the hallowed ground upon which he was standing to speak to the World which America says they were.

If any one man had instilled fear into his psyche in this world, it was Professor Spike Kaiser – one of the few Professors who refused to wear their beards. And that was each and every time that he spoke with him in the process of his discussions in defense of his Doctoral Thesis.

There were times when he felt that he had made the wrong choice of subject to write on.

There were times when he thought that he had made a great mistake to choose Maryland as the place for him to write his Thesis from.

There were times when he regretted having Professor Spike Kaiser as one of his Main Supervisors. Times when he came close to walking away from the Project on account of Professor Spike Kaiser's diatribes, jabs and acidic remarks.

Now to find that it was the same Professor Spike Kaiser who was the man showing his emotions to the point of his shouting to the roof tops in forgetting himself in hailing him for what he was saying.

Let us return to slide one of a few moments ago.

Yes, slide one! Thank you.

Slide two! Three! Eleven! Hold it there! He said as his Assistant moved his cursor from one slide to the next slide.

Go to slide forty! Hold it there!

There on that slide is the same man that we have on slide twenty two! The same man walking in a place that seemed to lead nowhere, here standing as though he is God The Maker of the World himself in frightful Military fatigue that he is wearing.

Go forward to slide forty seven! There he is the same man looking somewhere between the man he was in slide twelve and in slide forty about to transit to what we will see in our last slide.

What does it tell us? I mean the collective commulative picture that we have seen of everything that we have seen in all the slides?

What does it tell us?

Before I go any further, let me make clear that what we have seen is not anything taken from Will Rock my country of birth, my country of origin and the country that I love.

No! It is not about Will Rock. Neither is it about any country close to Will Rock. Nor is it about any known country in the whole wide world that we know.

It is about the concept of a country – it is only about a concept – the concept of the human condition which is only a condition of the mind and which can be seen in reality only by the mind that conceives it.

That Geography is there only because when we extrapolate all the images that we find in our fifty slides, what we see are not an approximation of the Fifty States that make up the United States of America!

No! They are an approximation of a country – many countries that we can find in many places, especially in Africa – Africa which is no longer a stranger to many people in the other Continents, and about which condition Uncle Sam is no longer ignorant except when he wants to be by choice – I mean deliberately.

It may include a country like Will Rock if we are honest with ourselves in the case of my dear Auntie Omagbemi, her little Companion Sola, who have just come from there and in whose mind the images that we have seen may be more graphic and truer than they will be in the minds of Olufemi Adedeji my brother in law, Demola Oloyode my brother, and even my treasure of a wife Abimbola my all and our twin Babies Bimbo and Jide!

A forest and a Sea of heads suddenly appeared somewhere in the middle of the Auditorium – all those being acknowledged standing up and clapping and waving spontaneously to be recognized by The Audience.

Everyone in the Audience clapped and stood up too to do what they had done throughout the hours that it had taken for Doctor Abejide Olanrewaju to speak – Standing Ovation.

Thank you Iya mi. Doctor Abejide said. Thank you my people! God bless you all!

# CHAPTER THIRTEEN

# HIDDEN MILLIONS UNVEILED

Now What Is The Role Of Ignorance in what we see and in what we are supposed to see but do not see In Third World – Underdeveloped Countries? He asked in his usual rhetoric once again.

This time Professor Spike Kaiser could not hold himself back any longer. He did, first, a quick march, and then ran almost as though he were a combination of Lindford Christie, Ben Johnson, Marion Jones and Usain Bolt.

He ran straight to the Podium and flung himself at Doctor Abejide Olanrewaju.

I am sorry to break Protocol. Professor Spike Kaiser said as he craned his neck to speak into the microphone far from where he stood.

When I muted the suggestion that we should tap our Speaker here for him to be the Resource Person to Speak at our Event today, I met a very stiff opposition whose Actors gave me more reasons than I could counter them, they being many, and I, being but one person.

They opposed me on many other Frontiers – Frontiers which they themselves broke down later when it began to dawn on them that I had spoken the truth as I knew it, no matter with what glasses they saw the image of the Speaker that they saw.

All those Opponents that I faced at the time in reference are here with us today!

They came here at their own volition in order for them to find reasons to agree with their earlier views or to disagree with me on the one hand, and on the other hand, for them to uphold what they have agreed with in the end.

They are the Decision Makers of my Proud State University of Maryland here in Baltimore!

They have on their own reached another far reaching Decision while yet the Speech is underway.

Let me, therefore, invite the President of the Senate of the State University of Maryland, Baltimore, Professor Jackson Texas for him to please step forward to make his monumental Announcement!

Professor Texas please!

Thank you, Spike! The ebullient Professor Jackson Texas said when he hurried to The Podium, almost panting for breath.

The Nobel must have started as result of the action of one man. Yes, the Nobel, just as anything else in the world started from the action or inaction of one man.

Were there a Nobel of some sort here in Maryland, we would give it to who you know. But we do not have a Nobel here. What we have is what has many things in common with the Nobel – Knowledge and the acknowledgement and Celebration of Knowledge!

The highest honour or accolade that any University Teacher can attain to is our own Brand of The Nobel here – Professor!

And so I, Representing all of us at The State University of Maryland, Baltimore, hereby invest Abejide Olanrewaju with the title of Professor of International Relations with effect from three days ago! Congratulations, Professor Abejaideei!

The Hall stood up on it's feet, the clapping and gyration deafening. Many people stormed the Podium, among them Lady Omagbemi and all of the persons who sat with her in her space.

Congratulations! Congratulations! Everybody sang, shaking hands with the Speaker and hugging him.

Ten people moved away from the maddening crowd and put their heads together for a while and then disengaged very quickly and moved back to their sitting positions.

Professor Jackson Texas came back to the Podium to speak, looking quite enthused.

We have one more announcement to make! He said, laughing.

We always had a Prize for our Best Graduating Students here in Maryland. Abejide won it at his Masters Degree Dissertation. But we held them back, hoping that he would stay on to go on to the *Pee Hetch Dee*.

He did to our great delight, but still, we waited. Now we cannot hold them back any longer.

We have saved the Dollars that went with the two previous Awards for the proud Winner.

We also know what the last one is worth too. Our newest Professor in all the world as I Speak here and now is Three Million Grand Richer!

Woo oo oo ooo ooo ooo ooo ooo ooo! The Auditorium exploded. Abejide quickly knelt down at the foot of the Podium. Lady Omagbemi, Bimbo, Olufemi, Demola, the twins – everyone in his Entourage joined him in that act of showing adoration, gratitude and praise worship to God – the act of kneeling down.

The Master of Ceremonies had a hell of a time asking for and getting the attention of the Audience. Every place seemed to be in disarray.

The Speaking Event that we came for has come to an unprecedented end – an end which I can tell you very authoritatively, was not pre-determined.

My Colleagues in the Media would call this Breaking News!

Every Guest should please head for the Luncheon which is available at five different locations within this same Coliseum of an Auditorium – The Quincy Adams Emporium. Please enjoy yourselves and have a good day! My Job is done!

Professor Abejide Olanrewaju could not eat a morsel, neither could he drink as much as a drop of water, nor could he drink a wine or Champagne. He just sat down and stared into space.

He had had too much of everything at the same time already where they were coming from.

He was grateful to God Almighty. He was grateful to God The Architect of The Entire Universe. Nothing happens in this world but by Him. He told himself.

He could publish the rest of his Speech along with what he had delivered already as a Book.

Yes, as soon as possible while the fire of Presentation was still hot inside him.

Yes. He should start writing right away. Yes. He should embark on that journey without wasting a second. There is a Market waiting for it. There is a ready Market – a huge Market waiting for it already!

What was he going to call it? What should he call it? He wondered as they drove back home to their Apartment in Femi's Luxury Space Wagon that looked in every way like The Greyhound Bus that thrilled Sola who would not want to accompany his Aunt – Auntie Omagbemi back home to Will Rock when it would be time for her – time for her, yes, and not time for the two of them to go back. He would not be part of that journey back in time to Will Rock. He was here to stay in America.

As Olufemi stepped on the accelerator of his Space Wagon, Lady Omagbemi burst into a hilarious praise song.

She had seen more than she expected to see. No. She was not going to wait until they got home. Olodumare Creator of The Entire Universe was mightily at work in her life here. His name must be praised. She told herself. He must be acknowledged instantly.

Bimbo did not wait for her to finish the first line of the song before joining her to sing –

> He has done for me,
> He has done for me …
> He has done for me,
> He has done for me …
> What my father
> Could not do,
> He has done for me …
> What my mother
> Could not do,
> He has done for me!

Olufemi Adedeji slowed down the vehicle that was sliding in bouncing movement as he himself joined in singing the song of Victory.

Who would want to be left behind in such a spontaneous outburst of sublime emotion in Magnifying, in Adoring, Glorifying, in Singing The Praise of The God of Miracles, The Giver of Every Good Thing In The Whole Wide World?

Demola Oloyode, not known for his singing abilities reached for whatever he could find to make his kind of percussion noise which he called his contribution to the music that was going on.

Sola and the Twins clapped and danced happily, the impact of what had happened to their Uncle and Dad not fully understood by any one of them.

Let us pull up at that McDonald's that I can see in front of us there, and give ourselves a drink in gratitude to God Almighty and in self adulation. Or is it ingratiation that I should call it? Ingratiation for what God Has done for us – for this unexpected turn of events? Professor Abejide Olanrewaju told Olufemi. We need to give thanks and offer praise worship to God Almighty even before we get home. He said. Home was too far away for them to wait for to start Adoring Him and to start Celebrating.

Here was Manner falling from Heaven and being given free and unexpectedly while they struggled and laboured to get just a chunk of meat and a piece of bread to eat from the evil hands of the devil and his Agents at work all over their space.

They were in for more surprises.

Every other car that was driving behind them also pulled up where they had pulled up as soon as they alighted from their own car.

# CHAPTER FOURTEEN

# A NOBEL FORETOLD

The newly crowned Professor Abejide Olanrewaju was invaded by a swarm of bees – human bees – an uncountable number of Journalists who were begging him for a chat with them on the events that they had gone to cover at The Quincy Adams Emporium.

They were sorry, they said, that he beat them to it by leaving the Venue before anyone of them knew it.

They would not take too much of his time, they pleaded with him. A very brief Interview without which their presence at the Ceremony would be completely meaningless. They told him.

Professor Abejide looked round the Members of his entourage as if to say Do you see my predicament? And they all seemed to understand. They would be a long way going home to their Apartment. There was McDonald waiting for them in the neighbourhood.

Before he knew it, Professor Abejide Olanrewaju was being powdered and given a face lift to face the Media, television lights shining bright as a Camp Fire all over him, Television Cameras focusing on him, Still Cameras clicking away at him and at Members of his entourage.

A very big Meet The Press Event was well underway also without anyone giving a thought to it earlier.

BERNARD STONEWALL

That's quite a sum of money to get in just over an hour, isn't it? I mean, Professor Jaide Olaniwaajuu, three Million Dollars, and nearly a half more in just over sixty minutes, isn't it?

ABEJIDE

Thank you, Sir. But before I go on to answer you, can you do me the favour of telling me your name, please?

BERNARD STONEWALL

I'm sorry, Professor! I am Bernard Stonewall of *The Dallas Eagle Radio And Tee Vee*. I'm sorry, I should have told you that before the question.

ABEJIDE

Thank you. My answer will be just as simple and as straight forward as your question. And I intend that it should go to every medium that is represented here as we are gathered, so that I do not have to address the same issue twice or seven times, the only difference being that they are being asked by Eagles or Hawks of DC or of Hollywood extraction. Now, you admitted it yourself that we were there where we are coming from, for more than fifty minutes. Are you telling me that throughout those fifty minutes, the only thing that made sense to you as the Eagle that you say that you are from Dallas and not Baltimore or anywhere near the State of Maryland, is the issue of money and how much it is justified or not justified for a fifty or sixty minute outing? Where did you keep your ears when the other Speakers spoke to illuminate the Hall and gave the reasons that they gave for the money that you are talking about? Or did you meet a stonewall there?

\*\*\*

There was an instant uproar. Nearly everyone laughed very loudly, including Bernard Stonewall himself. What a Poetic justice of an answer and a question all in one!

\*\*\*

## OAKWOOD JOE

My goodness! That was a terrific counter punch, Professor Abejaide! For the records, I am Oakwood Joe of the *Baltimore Times*. Were you satisfied that the Talk Shop ended the way it ended? That's my first question. Two. Would you have wanted to return to the Podium if you had been asked to go back? I am just wondering.

## ABEJIDE

I am going to answer this as the first question being asked here, not only because you write for The *Times of Baltimore*, but also because your question makes sense to me – makes more sense to me than what I heard before yours. I will answer you by first of all making a few assumptions. One. I hope that you were there in the Auditorium before I was invited to take to the stand? Two. I am going to assume that you did not leave the Auditorium from the time of the start of my Address to the time that we broke off for the Lunch Break from which we did not go back. With those two assumptions in mind, I will tell you how hungry I was to go back to rest my Speech. I was so desirous to go back to finish my Presentation that I did not drink any liquid, neither did I eat any food, nor did I do anything else except wait for to anchore the concluding part of that my Presentation.

I was like an Airplane ascending to Cruising Altitude to start flying in the Auto Mode when what happened happened suddenly, which, to me, was exactly like a Plane Crash, only that in this case, everyone On Board survived the crash, and with no damage being done to the Airplane itself.

No one has gotten to their destination yet, though. Not The Captain of the Flight. Not anyone of the Crew Members. Not anyone of the Passengers on Board.

I understand that no Pilot who survives a crash is ever allowed to fly again.

So, it is left for you to determine who the Captain of that our Flight was. Was it the Organizers of the Event?

Was it The Speaker of the day?

You decide that. The Good thing is that everyone is alive, hale and hearty.

And if in the end I am not labelled as the Captain of the Flight, I can fly again at any time that the Flight is ready to take to the skies again.

My Fifty Slides are still intact, as are my Computer Files.

Finally, I would very much have wished to conclude that my Presentation and taken enough questions from the Audience before leaving.

You know as well as I do know that you do not go against the will of the people without facing ugly consequences. You know that very well. Or don't you?

I did not bring the Presentation to an end myself. Other factors were responsible for that action.

I wonder if I have answered your question satisfactorily. If you think that I have not, I can go on and on –

OAKWOOD JOE

I am quite satisfied, Professor. Only, you know that everyone is an Oliver Twist of some sort.

ABEJIDE

I prefer an Oliver Twist to a tree with stunted growth. So, why not? You can go on!

OAKWOOD JOE

That's fantastic, Prof. This is a quick one. How would you describe the way that you felt after all the things that Royce Angelo, Professors Spike Kaiser and Jackson Texas said about you which culminated to the conflict Dollars?

ABEJIDE

Yes, Oakwood. You seem to lay credence to the fact that there has to be conflict in life for life to be worth living. Or isn't that the meaning of your reference to a very legitimate earing as conflict Dollars? Or is your Colleague's conflict with himself more meaningful to you than what is the truth that we all also know to be true? I don't expect you to respond. I will tell you how I felt and how I feel right now. I felt, first and foremost, grateful to God. Then I felt humbled to be so favoured. You were there, and so heard it like me and like everyone else, that a lot of what had happened in my association with the State University of Maryland here in Baltimore, was kept away from me until today. I am grateful to God that that was the case. For, who would imagine what I would have done with myself or what else I would have done, thereafter, if those monies had been given to me at the time that they should be given to me? Maybe the fortunes of my Doctoral would have been altered, and I may not have been the Speaker that I happened to be today. I am still trying to take in everything that has happened, including what has happened three weeks ago up to this day. I am humbled and look forward to justifying the appointment that I have been given as Professor in my Teaching and Research work at The SUM here. I feel good and very happy, indeed. There is no doubt about that.

LINDA RHODA

Professor Abejaide, I am Linda Rhoda. I am an Anchor with *The Canaan News Network.* Let me congratulate you for your promotion to the very well deserved Rank of General of The Army of The University! And for the beauty of your Presentation up until the time that it was terminated midstream! Your slides started with what you described as Void. Why did you start from that premise of a complete Void, Sir?

ABEJIDE

The Parley is getting more exciting, Linda! And by the way, thank you very much for congratulating me! As you know, you are the first person to do so! Yes. That is the truth, and I am touched by that humane gesture which takes me back to your question. In our world as it is in everything that you know, a Void always preceded anything that you ever did. And that is the way that it is going to be forever. For instance, you came here, not knowing what you would meet. Or did you know beforehand that everything that you have experienced here was going to be as it turned out to be?

That was a Void. Now, whatever you think of this my interaction with you, will also only act as something filling that Void in which you came here.

If I should stretch it further, we will also see very clearly that no one may build a house without first of all cutting the trees on the land, and clearing the land itself for it to fit into the pattern that the Architect and Building Engineers will find suitable for the actual construction phase to to start.

So it is also in Political Organizations.

Before you got on Board The CNN Train, you were interviewed during which period all there was, was a huge Void. Now, you are making the waves that you are making because you are filling the Void that was there before you got there, with the substance that you were when you appeared for the interview which discovered it and is the reason why you are flying as high and as sure as you are flying. But every Reporter or Anchor man or Anchor woman is not like you. Some Crash out after their very first story on the air. Some do not meet the expectations of the Media Organizations that engaged them only on the bases of their very impressive Cee Vees. Others break loose – break free and founded their own Organs of Expression after making their marks where they gave of their optimum. I guess I should stop here, especially as I ain't gonna get no dime for talking to you or to any one of your other colleagues for someone to ask me, thereafter, if it was justified or unjust!

BERNARD STONEWALL

Sorry Professor Abejanideei! Can I ask one more question? Thank you. If I tell you that I am honestly very sorry for the tone, texture and temper of my question, would you believe me, and forgive me, indeed? I ask this because I have come to the understanding after reviewing my earlier question all by myself that I shouldn't have started on that premise.

ABEJIDE

I am from a very solid Christian background, and believe in the Christian Faith being anchored on the tripod of Love, Charity and Forgiveness. I bear you no grudges after speaking my mind on the way that I felt. And so I hereby forgive you unconditionally, and short of reopening an old wound, want to assure you that I will contribute enough of my time and space to justify the Dollars that I have received today, which I did not quite expect. And so, why don't we draw the curtain on our interaction here?

BERNARD STONEWALL

I am fulfilled.

\*\*\*

The Media men and women began to pack their wares in readiness to leave.

***

ABEJIDE

Thank you, Gentlemen of The Press for respecting my feelings. I will hold all of you in very high esteem. Have a wonderful day!

PATTIE DAZZLE

Just one second, Sir! I am Pattie Dazzle! I write for the *Morning Sun Of Los Angeles*, and Host Celebrities for Hollywood Part Time! I am not about to ask you any question except if you ask me to ask you one. We have a tradition of thanking some of our Guests who make our time spent with them worth the while. We are of the view that you fit into that Sunshine! My sweet colleagues have picked me to appreciate you for the lucidity of your engagement with us.

Never mind that we did not all ask you questions.

We all listened in on the great conversation that you have held with us. And very attentively too. We all paid great attention to what you also took great pains to share with us. You were just awesome.

You were great when you spoke inside *Quincy Adams Emporium* as well as when you spoke to us out here. We are sure that what was hinted and copiously mentioned in that Hall, will come to you not long from now. Congratulations Professor Jaide! Congratulations!

ABEJIDE

Now, Miss Dazzle, are you just dazzling to humour me or to confuse me without telling me what you said you have told me and are congratulating me for in advance? Okay. Let me put it this way. You indicated that if I asked you to ask a question, you will oblige me and ask me a question.

That I remember very well. Yes, I remember that very well!

First, answer my question now.

And then you can go ahead to ask me whatsoever you will want to ask me. I will be very glad to answer you if I have the answers. But first, please tell me. And without any rigmarole or embellishments or whatever else you will call it.

What for are you congratulating me?

PATTIE DAZZLE

I Dazzle, Sir! I don't misdazzle! And I will love for us to agree on that before we go on.

***

Everyone giggled and laughed except Pattie Dazzle. She looked distraught.

***

PATTIE DAZZLE

Yes, Prof. I don't like being called Miss Dazzle. Pattie Dazzle is Okai – not Miss Dazzle! I don't like anyone calling me that waaaay!

ABEJIDE

I'm so sorry, Pattie Dazzle! I am hereby being properly informed. And now the answer to my question? Or is that also lost in the setting Sun?

PATTIE DAZZLE

O my Gad! Prof! You're so impossible! I don't know when I last laughed. Wait a minute, folks! We are all agreed, right? That our Guest, Professor Jaide is headed for The Nobel Prize For Literature? The second to go to Africa, is that right? Great? Prof. That's why I said Congratulations! Now you know. We hope to be there to cover it for all our Suns, Moons and Stars! You are a new Star on the Horizon that all of us can see very clearly. Have a wonderful day. Thank you! And so Congratulations once again!

ABEJIDE

Is that so? How many of you Think so? How many of you are you speaking for?

***

Then there was a forest of hands in the sky as nearly every Journalist there raised their hands to be counted along with Pattie Dazzle, including Bernard Stonewall, all of whom came to Professor Abejide Olanrewaju for a handshake.

***

ABEJIDE

I am flattered. Quite flattered! But see you at the very next opportunity, maybe at the Public Presentation of my Book. Very soon!

PATTIE DAZZLE

Wonderful, Prof! What are you calling it? And may I have the honour and the privilege to Preview it when you get to that stage?

ABEJIDE

You Dazzle me! But why not? That is very legitimate. *Stirring The Soul Of A Nation* is what I am thinking of calling it. In it, I will try to finish what I couldn.t quite finish in the Hall today. You know where to find me, anyhow, from Sunrise to Sunset, but here in Baltimore and not your City of Dazzling Angels!

PATTIE DAZZLE

Well said, Prof and Nobel Laureate! Here's my card. It's gat my phones and emails. Please call me when you're ready for me!

BIMBO

When the book is ready, Pattie! Not when he is ready for you!

PATTIE DAZZLE

O my Gad! I didn't think about that! I only meant to speak about the book! The Book, Madam. And naatin else!

BIMBO

I perfectly understand, Pattie! I understand. Perfectly. I mean perfectly!

PATTIE DAZZLE

I hope so, Madam!

# CHAPTER FIFTEEN

## STIRRING THE SOUL OF A NATION

In less than ten or so minutes after those engaging moments of questions, answers, comments, observations, disagreements and agreements, the Parking Arcade of The McDonald's on the Highway leading to the residence of the new Professor in town Abejide Olanrewaju was almost deserted, with all of the Journalists gone.

Can you picture in your mind what would have happened? Professor Olanrewaju said, directing his observation at his brother in law Olufemi Adedeji who had left Will Rock their home country for the longest time. If what happened here during the last one hour or so ago had taken place in our country?

Nope! Olufemi Adedeji said, his eyes wide open in naked expression of surprise. What do you mean to say? He asked his in law the newly robbed Professor.

O yes! Professor Olanrewaju said in excitement. Now is the time you will see this place full of people. All the foreign Correspondents would be gone – yes, gone just as they have gone quickly away from here to go and file their stories. But all the indigenous Journalists would be hanging around stampeding me with otiose and annoying questions like So how do we go from here? What do you have for us? When are we going to wash the Professor Title? Where is it going to take place? Even the Editors, even Editors-In-Chief, and, in some cases, the Managing Partners of the Publishing Houses and Electronic Outfits.

None of them will lay premium on the need for them to go to town with the News Contents that they have received. They will be pestering me with requests for gratification – bribe money in plain language, Femo ooo ooo, yes!

In some cases the same thing will be said in hidden Parables or given sweet names such as Transport Fares and Lunch Monies for it to sound good and legitimate.

Some of them would also have made huge Orders for food here and gone away with them as Take Aways after pointing at me to the Salesmen and to the Saleswomen as the man who would pay for what they have carted away! Yes, without letting me know that they were going to do so before doing it. They would take it for granted that I would pay.

Really? Olufemi Adedeji asked in horror and disbelief as he stood akimbo.

O yes! That's what you would have seen here if we had done what we have done here back at home.

Incredible! I can't believe it! Olufemi Adedeji said.

You better believe it. Professor Olanrewaju said, almost shouting. And the worst part of it is that if you fail to yield to those their arm twisting tactics or sickening and outrageous demands, they will black you out of the news. They will not mention anything about the event that has taken place, no matter how monumental it may be. That's how bad it is. That's the situation we face at home. They will say they have black listed you and will vow not to attend any other Event concerning you.

My Jove! Olufemi Adedeji exclaimed, shaking his head in disbelief as he tried to take in what he had been told. They were as he said incredible but true. That was the stark reality that people faced, not only in Will Rock but in almost all the countries on the African Continent.

Here. He said. Somebody is going to get fired, if they are proven to have collected a dime – just a dime as gratification money! That's what's gonna happen here. He said breaking into the typical American way of speaking by reflex. They' ll get fired even if they only suggested it.

I know! I know, Fem ooo ooo! Professor Abejide Olanrewaju said as he walked over to where Lady Omagbemi was sitting with his wife Abimbola, their twins Bimbo and Jide Junior and Demola Oloyode.

Hey, Iyawo mi! He called his wife, laughing broadly – Iyawo mi meaning in Yoruba My darling wife. Was that not a bit harsh on that Miss Dazzle? He asked his wife, pretending to pant for breath. Ha! I was afraid that she could explode, you know! He said. I was quite afraid ooo ooo.

I needed to warn her in good time, Darling! Abimbola said. These people! I have heard a lot of stories about them before today. And that is one of their tactics. They start by appearing to be very nice and business-like. And harmless. But before you know it, the damage is done. And you begin to regret not speaking up at the time that you should have spoken up loud and clear. That's what I was trying to do, my dear husband – ee ee ee? The newest Professor in all the world!

But she was very graceful in the way she took it. Lady Omagbemi said, shaking her head as she picked the boneless Chicken from the plastic plate in front of her. She took it very well. And if she ever had any dreams before about what was not in the record books, now she knows. They are all bloody Cowards too. Nearly all of them. Especially when you give it back to them and stand up to what you have said the way that you did it.

Lady Omagbemi sunk her two front teeth in the breast of Chicken she had picked up earlier with the aid of the two lower teeth, her eyes partially closed to prevent pepper from popping out into them to hurt her and mellow down her huge appetite, and then, shook her head in acknowledgment of the sweet taste of the Chicken McDonald's. She then put the rest of what was left of the Chicken back into the plate in front of her. But be careful, Bimbo. She said facing her in-law. Be very careful next time you are faced with such a temptation. Jide is a very good boy. He will not fall for their antics. That I can assure you from what I know him to be after these many years that he has spent with me. And sometimes, you have to keep what you feel inside of you inside of you – yes, inside of you, especially at such Ocean-wide arenas. It could be quite dangerous. Yes. I am telling you what I know very well.

I am sorry, Ma. Bimbo said, standing up to genuflect for the Matriarch Omagbemi, indicating that she would not do the same thing again if she were to face the same circumstance again, no matter where.

Iya ooo ooo! Professor Abejide Olanrewaju exclaimed, Iya ooo ooo meaning Grand wife, Grand mother or Grand Matriarch or Grand anything good, to suggest that she had spoken with the wisdom of Solomon and with the bravery of the lion without giving a thought to how badly the Ox was gored or how the Ox would feel the pain of the attack of goring.

Lady Omagbemi laughed like a baby, remembering her younger days when she would have disappeared into thin air to feather her own nests in one of the many forests of Lucrative America, leaving her Hosts and Hostesses to pilot their own Airplane their own way where they were or wherever they chose to be.

She knew that she was in a situation that was dire and unchangeable. It was like the mirror image of an object being desired or detested which someone saw on the canvass of their minds. No one else can ever see it exactly as the person seeing that image would see it. Neither can anyone change or alter it. Nor can anyone do anything about it's presence on that panorama where it was fixed. It was there, and there the way that it was, no matter what happened or did not happen.

# CHAPTER SIXTEEN

# THE WILL OF GOD NO MAN OR WOMAN CAN ALTER

The families of the new Professor in all the world had a wonderful time watching very generous live telecast of the Public Lecture from which they had made tremendous gains –Financial gains, Political gains, Social gains, Academic gains, Spiritual gains. What else? Everything! Yes, everything.

When one News Network showed Lady Omagbemi kneeling down on the floor shedding tears and holding Professor Abejide Olanrewaju by his waist, and his wife Abimbola doing the same thing with the twins wiping the tears from all three of them, including from the face of their father, the three people broke down in tears once again by seeing the emotions that they had displayed before.

Oma se e ooo ooo! Olufemi exclaimed, what he said meaning It is pitiful or What a pity, patting all of them at their shoulders as he looked from them to the images of them that the silver screen was showing to them.

You know. Lady Omagbemi said as she wiped the tears from her own eyes. Certain tears of joy are more genuine and are also more painful than tears that you cry in pain from a terrible thing that has happened to you. Why would I not shed tears? Why would I not? Who would have thought or believed that Jide had all these potential hidden inside him? What if we could not raise the money to make his journey to come here possible? Just imagine what we would have lost! Three Million United States Dollars! And even more because Jide told me that they even paid him separately for the Lecture that he went there to deliver because the doors of Heaven had begun to open! Why would we not shed tears? Well done, Jide. Well done! I am very proud of you! Well done! And thank you, Abimbola for believing in him right from day one. Thank you. Jide did not hide anything from me. He told me everything. He told me everything that you people passed through to get here. Everything. He told me about all his fears and his frustrations. He told me about all his handicaps and inadequacies. He told me how all through those moments of doubts and uncertainties you encouraged him like the mother – yes, like the proud mother that you are now by the Special Grace of *Olodumare*. What am I going to say about my proud in law Olufemi? He was graceful. He was loving. He was forward looking and quite magnanimous! He said to you My dear Sister Come! Come and stay with me here in America before people see your stomach bulging out to begin to wag their tails and to begin to gossip up and down. He said keep that your pregnancy! And allowed Jide to also come and join you here to stay with him in his own house happily. If any of these bits of our long story had happened differently, would we have been where we are today? We will not! And everything boils down to the Will of God Almighty Which no one can alter. Thank you, *Olodumare*! I thank you with all my heart, sinner that I am! She said as the tears came back again and this time in greater torrents than it did flow before.

This time Olufemi Adedeji himself cried, touched by the history which Lady Omagbemi had graphically painted on the Panorama of the past and the present on the Canvass in front of them that were very clear for everyone to see – even those who were not there where some of the episodes of the drama happened.

Lady Omagbemi remembered the man she married who had died many years ago. She also remembered his childhood friend Bolaji who had taken her over, and had been a strong tower of support for her and for her Ward Abejide Olanrewaju who he loved to call Deji. She remembered the moment at which she had described herself as a whore to his chagrin on the day that they had held a special meeting for her to place the problem that she was facing in Abejide needing to make his trip to the United States of America – money and other obstacles being the problem which she had found to be insurmountable.

No one else knew what was going on in the turmoil of her mind as she cried.

Tears were all that they saw and could see. Tears, and nothing else.

That was part of the mystery and the greatness of the Creation Engineering Adequacy of *Olodumare, Tamuno* in Kalabari, *Bari* in Ogoni or *Chineke* in Igbo.

That no one sees what lay buried in any person's mind – in any other person's mind but is as stormy as *Katrina* in the mind of someone else standing shoulder to shoulder with you.

Olufemi Adedeji was persuaded to stay the night there with the weeping but very happy family – a family weeping over their recollections of what they had passed through side by side the huge miracle of God in the life and fortune of one of them – Professor Abejide Olanrewaju the man because of whom they were all in Baltimore at this point in time.

Demola Oloyode being a Baltimore Resident himself, picked his way back home very late at night, very happy with his little contribution to the success and outcome of the events of the day.

God. He said before he left. Does not forget anybody. And He has a special day for everyone that He Created.

True. Everyone said in agreement with him.

Time ticked on mercilessly and endlessly tirelessly on it's journey into forever and eternity without missing a beat.

One late afternoon, Lady Omagbemi, Professor Abejide and his wife Mrs. Abimbola Olanrewaju were doing what they called Window Shopping which was to lead them on to eating of an early Dinner outside their home as part of their Package to let her have as much fun as possible before her return home to Will Rock in a fortnight when Olufemi Adedeji telephoned to say that he was heading for their Apartment to give his sister information that they had all been waiting for a long time before that date for to receive.

He had arrived in Baltimore at the Head of a Team of Technical Experts to look at his Company's possible involvement in another Construction Company's Mega Project, but the meeting had come to an abrupt end with news of the Principal Partner losing his ailing mother in a Specialist Hospital in The City of New York and who had had to catch a Flight to the scene of disaster in a hurry, leaving him all the time in the world to spare. The three people came to a quick agreement that Abimbola should go and meet her brother to receive the information which he was bringing for her. If he had time on his hands after they finished discussing and also felt favourably disposed to accompanying her to the place where she broke off from them to go and meet him, he should please accompany her back to the place that they were, for them to eat the Dinner which they had arranged to eat before his arrival, they agreed.

Abimbola's driving had greatly improved. And so she took to the wheels, and soon was gone tearing away on the free way to their Apartment.

Good. Lady Omagbemi said. You know it would have been rude and improper for me to ask to go out from your Apartment with you for us to do or discuss anything without your wife accompanying us. She told Professor Abejide Olanrewaju.

Yes, Auntie. He said. That is very true.

Good. She said. Because after you are officially legally married, with the twins and the next set of twins that are on the way, I understand, by the way, you have, as the Bible says, become one flesh. But there is still need for an older sister to have private discussions with her younger brother. Just like the two of us, I mean. She said, pointing at him and at herself with the forefinger of her right hand.

I quite understand. He told her, shaking his head in complete agreement with her in what she had said.

Jide. She said as she sat down near the Lobby of the Shop that they were looking in. One Million Dollars is a lot of money by today's standards, anywhere in the whole wide world. It is a lot of money even here where it has it's mother and it's father whether they call them Uncle Sam or Brother Samuel. They worship him too. Yes, Americans all worship The Dollar in which they Trust even more than in God! Money means everything to them.

I understand, my dear Aunty. Abejide said, still shaking his head.

You have three. Lady Omagbemi said, smiling beautifully. You have three complete Million Dollars! I know very well that you have thought about all the things that you want to do with it, if as I also know and believe, you are still the same Jide that I have known from early childhood. Therefore, all I want to know is what some of those plans that you have made or which you are still tinkering with are. And whether I can make any input or suggestions or not. I have been waiting for the perfect opportunity to say this. And thank goodness, this is it where Bimbo is out of our space for good reasons.

Aunty. Professor Abejide Olanrewaju called her in a very affectionate manner. You see. He said. This is why even way back at home, not many people know up to this moment that you are not my biological mother. When I cry for her sometimes – I mean when I cry sometimes that my actual mother is no longer here with me, it is not because I lack motherly care, love and attention, but because I would have wanted for her to be here with us as the third person to share our joys and sorrows with us the way it was that I remember when she was around. That is just why, and nothing else. You are a great mother of an Aunty.

Ah! Omo ooo ooo mi Lady Omagbemi called him most adoringly, saying What a lucid way of expressing the truth, my dear son! This is why you see me shed tears many times too even when, at those moments, what I should be doing is jubilate. You have spoken very well. So what plans do you have in the works to add value to the money that God has mercifully given to you? She asked him, looking away from him for dramatic effect. People spoke their minds best when they know that no one was peering into their eyeballs. She knew very well.

Professor Abejide Olanrewaju kept quiet for a fairly long time. He would have remained silent for a much longer time than he did, if not for his consideration and understanding that Abimbola his wife would be on her way back there any time from that time. They needed the space of her absence to conclude what they were discussing before she returned.

He unfolded his plans to Aunty Omagbemi just as he would do to his biological mother if she had been the person who had asked him what Lady Omagbemi – Aunty that she was to him, had asked him at that material time. He also felt proud of himself as he told her what he laid bare to her – the plans which he had carefully drawn up to execute here and way back home in Will Rock.

A huge Shelter back at home in Will Rock was on the Card. He told her. A smaller Shelter in Ekiti their permanent home was there. He told her that A huge Farm – An Integrated Farm Settlement in Ekiti which would produce livestock and foodstuff on a very massive scale was also on the Card. Here in Baltimore, Maryland, he would Build a Modest House for his family which would put an end to their payment of Rents – a House which he could put up for sale whenever they were returning home for good or leave it as it would be, for it to provide Shelter for him and for anyone else who visited from home in the future that was going to be there permanently.

He would build another House in the same State of Maryland which he would use for A Museum of African Art which people would visit to pay money to see what he would put there, but none of which Artifacts would be sold.

He would attach a Supermarket to it as well as a Guest House to accommodate ten persons at a time with Facilities to provide African Dishes or Cuisine at a modest fee to attract a large Clientele and Patronage.

Wonderful! Wonderful, my dear son! Lady Omagbemi screamed in spite of herself and in spite of the environment they were in where people milled around as though they had no other places to go to apart from wandering about there. She was totally satisfied with his plans.

You have covered every Chapter and Verse from all the Books of The Old Testament to the last Book, Chapter and Verse in The New Testament. She told him, laughing. You have gone from Genesis to Revelation, almost as though the two of us had sat down to discuss this long before now. Congratulations! All I can do for you now is to put you in my Daily Prayers that everything that you have planned to do should succeed according to your vision and according to God's Perfect plan.

Amin! Professor Abejide said very loudly, Amin meaning the same thing as Amen.

He would open a Special Bank Account for her there in Baltimore which she would draw from in Ocean View City in Will Rock to execute the home based Projects that he had talked about, as soon as possible.

He would personally supervise the Projects based on American Soil. That should happen a few days before her journey back home – Opening of the Special Bank Account for her. He said.

She would go back home with a MasterCard that would work anywhere in the whole wide world to make Funds' Withdrawals and Expenditures on the pet Projects that they had agreed to execute easy and be a thing of delight as well as to assure Lady Omagbemi herself of her own up keep.

Abimbola and Olufemi were around in the Mall where The Supermarket in which they were waiting was situated, Professor Abejide Olanrewaju and Lady Omagbemi were informed.

It was Professor Abejide Olanrewaju who answered the telephone call that came in from his wife Bimbo at that point in time on which she told him that her brother Olufemi who she had gone to meet was also there on the Grounds of the Mall with her.

He and Lady Omagbemi his Aunty were walking out from where they were sitting waiting for them before to meet them. Professor Abejide Olanrewaju told her.

As the four people tied together by family strings sat to eat the long arranged Dinner outside the shores of their homes nearby and far away from where they were, there was no word spoken or coughed about the very important and long awaited information which the only brother there had brought for the only sister there – Olufemi and Abimbola.

Whether any one of Abejide and his wife Abimbola expected for the other person to be the one to open discussions on that subject or not, no one knew. And there was no way for anyone knowing about the truth of that matter which everyone was also very happy to sweep under the carpet. Silence could be golden at certain times. Times such as now.

Afterall, here on the American Soil, there was a Provision in the Constitution called Amendment which granted the right to any and every Citizen for them to keep completely mum on any issue that they did not feel obliged to speak on, even if they were asked to do so by the Highest Court of the Land – The Supreme Court, whether that Amendment was called Second or Fifth Amendment did not quite matter.

# CHAPTER SEVENTEEN

## TEARFUL GOODBYE AS LADY OMAGBAMI GOES BACK HOME TO WILL ROCK

Doctor Ferdinando Shepherd was unusually egregious on this Sunday Morning when he announced to his Flock of Sheep that they were hosting a Visiting African Settler Family to their Thanks Giving to God Almighty The ever Faithful Provider of every good thing in the world for the great works which He had worked in their lives for they and The Good Lord only knew how long. He said, laughing – laughing, which was also something very unusual for anyone to see him do, no matter how happy or joyous the task of the Good Shepherd that he performed in imitation of the Author and Finisher of The Faith, and in justifying the pay that he received in performing those duties religiously, that unlike several situations like that which they had seen happen time and time again, on this particular occasion, it would be the mother, and not the father of the Quartet who would speak to inform the Congregation as to why they were doing what they had come to do.

Let me, therefore, with great gratitude to The Good Lord, invite Mrs. Abimbola Olanirewajuu, wife of the Scholar who was inducted into the Hall of Fame of Professors while at a Podium Delivering a Speech that stirred the soul of our nation, Abejaiday, to please come forward to share their thoughts of the greatness of Gaad with us His faithful Servants in His Vineyard. Misses Olanirewajuu please!

The clapping went on for more than five minutes as the humble woman of Ekiti Dynasty in far away Will Rock waited to break the ice that was hot in her heart.

Praaiiiiissssss the Looorrrrrrrd! She screamed three times with her eyes firmly shut and her vocal chords stretched to their limit.

Hallelujah The Faithful's responded all three times, the Church instantly energized.

I see it as The Lord's own doing that my dear husband Jide known for making great Speeches all across the land, would on such a momentous occasion of our showing gratitude to God The Creator of The Universe and all of us men and women, ask me to be the one speaking about all the wondrous works that He has done for us in our lives from as far back in time as we can remember to the recent past that we know.

May I, with the humility of The Good Shepherd kneel in His Presence and before all of you present here, therefore, to Thank Him and also to thank my wonderful and faithful husband Jide for this opportunity and privilege as I Praise His Holy Name with this song that I was taught to sing very early in my childhood. I will sing the first two stanzas now and sing the last stanza at the end of the story we have come to share with you. It is called He Is There, Here and Everywhere For You!

When you wake
In the morning
And see the sun
Come shining
Out of the clouds,
That is
The Good Lord
Smiling at you,
Bestowing
His Favours
On you and all
He brought
Into being.
Halleluiah!

When you see
The clouds darken
In the evening
As the sun begins
To fade
And to disappear,
Do not despair
That He has left you –
No. He is
Still there
Behind
The darkest clouds
And everywhere.
Rejoice! Rejoice!

She sang in a voice so sonorous and mellifluous that were the glass work with which the Church Auditorium was decorated not of the firm alloy that they were made of, it could tear through them and spill outside the precinct of the Church itself, resonating shrill and sweet.

The Congregation clapped to applaud her.

Abimbola tried hard to fight the tears that she knew were anxious to fall from her eyes. She … she pleaded with the tears. Please stop … she said as she waited for the ovation to die down.

While the clapping lasted, as had been rehearsed earlier, Professor Abejide Olanrewaju walked the rest of the Members of the Quartet and their Affiliates to the sides of his wife, left and right.

On my immediate right is Jide the Head of our humble home –

She was interrupted at that point by thunderous cheers and clapping while the man being introduced bowed round about him and waved at all the Four Corners of the Church.

Thank you. She said to both her husband for keeping to their agreed path to follow, and to the Congregation for applauding him, and then continued her Speech.

The fight against the tears also continued, making her feel helpless.

To Jide's immediate right is my elder brother, Brother Olufemi Adedeji who flew in from Atlanta, Georgia to be with us on this our Special occasion today.

Brother Femi, by the way, was our first Host here in the States when Jide and I arrived on these beautiful Lands six years ago!

The ovation was just as thunderous as it was for her husband, if not even louder than before.

Olufemi bowed just as his brother in law did and waved at the Congregation too, laughing broadly. Lady Abimbola looked at him with untainted joy and satisfaction.

In front of us here are our first Gifts from Him above and our blessings here below, little Bimbo and Jide who made our joy complete!

The twins all turned to give their Parents a hug while the Congregation applauded them clapping and saying Hoo-hoo-hoo-hoo-hoo-hoo!

Finally, my dear brethren in the Lord, is my mother and my husband's great Auntie, the very well loved and respected Lady Oma Gbemi!

She called the name Omagbemi as if it were two words Oma and Gbemi. She did so for very special dramatic effect which was not lost on the Matriarch of honour.

The Congregation did not allow her to finish her introduction.

They gave Lady Omagbemi a standing ovation, shouting Ho-ho-ho-ho-ho- ho-ho-ho-ho-ho!

The Matriarch blushed as she waved smiling beautifully.

Our dear Mommy who has been here with us for the past three weeks which have flown past like three short days, is unfortunately also leaving for home with little Sola here, even before we have finished saying welcome to them, also three short days from today. Sola wave –wave to the people! She advised the little boy called Sola in an aside who waved mechanically and in no given order. He covered his face with his two hands bashfully.

Lady Abimbola turned left to hug Lady Omagbemi from whose eyes the River began to flow again, making her own fight a lost battle.

Tears, tears, but why? Abimbola wondered.

Lady Omagbemi genuflected and waved with her two hands to the Congregation saying Thank you, Thank you in subdued whispers.

There was a moment of freeze as the Lady Abimbola the Toast Master hid her face behind Lady Omagbemi to cry her heart out.

Everyone who saw those tears saw them for what they were – Tears of great joy – joy beyond all understanding.

Doctor Ferdinando Shepherd, more used to dealing with sadness and emotional break downs than happy times, stepped down from the Holy of Holies where he sat and threw a gentle pat at the backs of Lady Omagbemi and all the people standing in front of the Congregation, and then moved away silently and unobtrusively.

Misses Abimbola Olanrewaju talked about the Doctor of Philosophy Degree which her husband had earned not long ago in the City of Baltimore in the State of Maryland. Which they have come to love with uncanny passion.

She talked about the Speaking opportunity that he was given while defending his Thesis, and ended the Chapter on him with his Investiture as Professor of International Relations in the full glare of the world as well as the announcement of his Headship of the new Department of Afro American

Studies at the State University of Maryland as Acts which only The Good Lord could perform to His own Glory and Edification.

She extolled the warmth as well as the virtues of Lady Gbemi who she said they wished would stay with them, if not forever, but for longer.

She ended her Speech by singing the last stanza of the song with which she opened the Curtain of her performance as she had indicated earlier in her very well Packaged delivery, notwithstanding all the hiccups, fits and starts that were occasioned by the Oceans of tears that cascaded down the hearts of the grateful Family of Four and their supporters.

> Rejoice,
> Flower
> In His hands
> In the morning
> And chick
> Under His wings
> In the evening
> And all through
> The night.
> He is there with you.
> He is here for you
> All the way through
> Your life's
> Every endeavour!

Doctor Ferdinando Shepherd said Lady Abimbola Olanrewaju had made his job very easy for him. She had in fact done it for him fully. He said.

God The All knowing. He said. Would continue to uphold those who laid all their cares on Him and worshipped Him in Spirit and in Truth.

He referred to the Family standing before them as a shining example of what the favour of God could do for a people who believed in Him, and enjoined every Faithful to walk the path of moral rectitude and Sowing bountifully in God's own Vineyard.

His prayer was very brief and straight to the point as he laid hands on all the Family Members kneeling before him from one person to the other while it lasted, but with his two eyes wide open all the while that he prayed.

He prayed for journey mercies for Lady Omagbemi and little Shooola as they travelled back home to Will Rock on Wednesday, and asked for The Favour of The Good Lord to rain ceaselessly on the Family Openly Declaring His Faithfulness to His Church, Praising, Magnifying, Worshipping and Adoring Him for His Mysterious ways.

The Choir sang The Hymn O God Our Help In Ages Past, and with their widow's mites safely placed in the gold plated Tray placed on the Table in front of the Lectern, the Thankful family retired to their seats.

Doctor Shepherd's Sermon too was very brief. It was almost as short as the shortest Verse in the whole Bible that read And Jesus Wept.

Call upon The Lord in times of despair! As well as in your best of times! And He will rescue you! As well as Hear you! He said. And that was all he said.

And the Service came to an end. Wonderful. Wonderful. Many of the Faithfuls said, admiration and relief – in very welcome relief.

There was a fairly elaborate Reception on the Grounds of the Lord Emmanuel Baptist Church, Baltimore, fondly called and known as LEBC.

Only a handful of close friends and Associates accompanied the Family to their Residence for the continuation of the Happy Celebrations.

Professor Abejide Olanrewaju declared one day of Fasting for them to pray for journey mercies for Lady Omagbemi and little Sola, beginning from midnight that Sunday.

And it was in that spirit of Fasting and waiting upon the Lord that Lady Omagbemi, accompanied by Mrs. Abimbola Olanrewaju went to the Bank of America Branch very close to their Apartment in Baltimore to Open her New Bank Account, and was issued her Platinum MasterCard almost immediately. She could cash money in any part of the Planet wherever there was a Bank.

While there were loud laughters and hilarious hugs as well as frenetic hops from one Entertainment Spot to the other at the Arrival Lounge of The Baltimore International Airport and in the surrounding neighbourhood on the day Lady Omagbemi arrived with Sola to begin her visit, on the Wednesday of their departure, the atmosphere was so different and so cloudy that the tears that the Family cried nearly drowned the runway of the Airport to make take off of Airplanes impossible.

The most pained among the people from whose eyes the tears rained was little Sola who realized too late that his prayers for him to be allowed to stay back in America for Lady Omagbemi to go back home alone, had not been granted.

Don't worry. Professor Jide Olanrewaju told him. You' ll come again very soon. We will come and see you too. He said.

Little Sola brightened up on hearing what his uncle had just told him, asking Will Bimbo and Jide also come with you when you are coming? Bimbo and Jide referring to the twins with whom he had bonded beautifully during his candle brief stay with them.

With one last wave from the Travellers and from those who had been being visited, Lady Omagbemi and Sola disappeared into the restricted Area For Flyers Only.

Moments, thereafter, Professor and Mrs. Olanrewaju could see the Delta Airlines Big Bird Soaring into the bright sunny skies smoothly dancingly.

A greatly anticipated visit had come and gone, leaving in it's wake but tears and sweet memories, in some cases, painful memories and dreams unfulfilled.

# CHAPTER EIGHTEEN

# WINNER ALL THE TIME – WHY

When Abimbola woke from her deep sleep in the dark of that early Thursday morning, she was surprised that Abejide her husband was not by her side on the bed. She turned on the light and saw on the clock hanging opposite her on the wall that it was only past 2:00 Am.

She left the dim lights on for a reasonable length of time during which she let her mind wander from one thought process to the other.

She tried to remember what she dreamt of which had led to her suddenly waking up but could not remember any bit of what had happened in that world of illusion.

It is just as well. She thought to herself.

Then she got angry but without knowing what for she was angry.

She tried to turn to the left side of her frame from her lying position but felt severe pains by the mere effort to turn.

Ah! She hissed. Those twin babies were the cause. She told herself. She pointed her anger in the direction of her husband all of a sudden.

Why was he not by her side to provide her with the emotional support that he should provide her in these times of her ordeal which she was going through for the second time in their lives together on account of what the two of them did by choice and very happily? She wondered. Why was he not there? Why was he not there by her side?

It was the law of nature, yes, that the women should bear sole responsibility for carrying the babies in their wombs for nine months each and every time that pregnancy happened. She reflected. Yes. Yes. Ah! Yes.

Yes, but each and every time that that accident or that Mystery of the Science of Creation occurred, the women were only the Vessels – they were only the Mediums carrying the Products, while the men were also always responsible for sowing what they carried on the long Journey to the Ports of Delivery.

And, therefore, even if the man did not see himself as the Captain of the Ship ahoy – the Ship on the move on the Waters of time, he should at least see himself as being a very good Pathfinder to Guide her on the path that the Ship Sailed, providing her with water when she was thirsty, providing her with food when she was hungry and providing her with fuel when she needed to be re-fuelled for the health and well being of the people unseen that she carried in her womb and for her emotional release.

She knew where her husband was. Yes, Abimbola told herself. She knew where he was. No doubt about it.

I know where he is. She told herself. He must be at his writing desk in his Study studying or writing. Writing or Studying. Studying or Writing. But why? Studying what? What was he Studying or Writing?

No. She told herself. He has no business staying anywhere else except by my side! He has to be by my side. And now! She told herself. Now. Not, later.

She would go and disturb him – pull him away from his books and pen. He must give her some attention this morning. Whatever he was reading or writing can wait, and should wait! Yes, at this time of this day – this early morning. And her musing continued.

He has received his Doctorate, afterall, and has moved way beyond where others may not get to even after ten years of Research Work and Teaching. Is that not the truth? Yes, it is! Yes! That is the truth.

What else did he have to prove to himself or to the world? She queried angrily inside of her as she began to take her heavy frame out of the broad bed, one leg at time, one hand at a time, beginning to feel feverish out of her feeling of desperation and abandonment.

Good Morning, Jide. She greeted him in a very faint voice after she tip toed into his Study to see him scribbling away just as she had guessed.

Ah! He exclaimed with fear and with worry in his face. Ah! Iyawo mii – my dear wife. He said.

He put the pen he held in his right hand down on the table and got up to go and meet her, his legs wobbly, trembling and unsure.

He hugged her tenderly and gave her a peck on her forehead.

Come and sit down. He told her, leading her to his writing table where he pulled out the Chair that he sat on before her arrival for her to sit on it. He gave way for her to have plenty of leg room to relax and to feel very comfortable.

She sat down and stretched her two legs in pain – pain which he felt in his heart, feeling sorry for being responsible for what she was going through, wishing that he could take part of the burden that she bore in order to make it lighter for her to bear her own bit. But he knew that that was not possible. It was against the law of Nature. He could only feel it in his considerate heart.

Did you miss me? He asked her as he placed his right hand over her left shoulder.

She looked up into his eyes and laughed, asking inside of her Are you asking me? That I missed you? She began to speak.

I wanted to make sure that you were okay yourself. She told him, placing her own right hand over his right hand which was still on her left shoulder. Her hand looked heavy on him. He thought.

That was very thoughtful of you. He said. Aren't you a treasure of inestimable value to me? He asked her. While I should be the person bothering about your well being and in your state of health, heavy as you are, it is you who you are so caring, so thoughtful and so mindful of my own well being that you have had to cut your sweet sleep to come here and ask after me, and to make sure that I was fine? Isn't that wonderful? Thank you, darling. I am so proud of you and so happy I married you that I am just wondering what life would have been for me without you by my side.

He reached for the side stool at the far end of the Study and went to sit beside her, resting his head on her right side.

I can see why you are a Winner all of the time. She said. I can see why. She repeated, and then held him with her two hands very tenderly. Why do you say so? He asked her, rubbing her stomach with his left hand to try to put her at greater ease than he thought that she was. What have you seen as my winning formula, *Iya mii?* He asked her, *Iya mii* meaning My dear mother, but here said very emotionally dearly. And the effect was not lost on her. She felt very good inside of her.

Jide. She called him softly, turning her head from the left to the right hand side very slowly, her lips drawn together as though she were about to whistle or to spit saliva out of her mouth. She closed her eyes as though she was going to pray.

I was in very serious pains when I managed to walk in here. She said. I woke up suddenly from sleep because of what I saw in a dream that I was dreaming. When I felt for you with my left hand on the bed and found out that you were not there, I felt very unhappy and even angry – very angry. I came here to fight you, Honey … Jide, I came here to fight you because I felt abandoned. But look at your reaction to just seeing me in your space – this your Study. Look at where I am sitting, and where you are sitting – owner of the entire space that you are! How can my anger endure? How can I say that I will fight you again? This is why I said I can see why you are always a winner because you are always so considerate, you are always so careful, always so caring and faultless in the way that you do everything that you do that it will be difficult, if not outright impossible for anyone to get the better of you. I am so proud of you – so proud of you that I don't know just as you yourself said a few moments ago, what my life would have been like for me, If I were to have someone else, and not you, in this my space and in this my condition. God bless you, *Baba beji.* She said, hugging him tearfully, *Baba beji* meaning Father of Twins.

Professor Abejide Olanrewaju was speechless. He helped his wife to get back to her feet.

And in the next few moments, they were back to their Bed Room together.

# CHAPTER NINETEEN

# PRODUCT OF AN ACCIDENT

This book is the product of an accident. And what is an accident? Professor Abejide Olanrewaju was asking himself as he read from the page of the printed words in front of him in answer to the Media Personality who was sitting opposite him in the very large Study of his Office as Head of Department of the School or Institute of Afro American Studies of the State University of Maryland in Baltimore. Give you a copy? No. Not yet. I'm not there yet. Not there yet. He said. We are gonna get there, I know, but we are not there yet.

That's okaiii! The Lady sitting opposite him said. Sometimes we have listened to great Writers read their works to us from the first page to the last page as part of the process of Introducing the works to the Reading Public. We gaat a whole lot of books like that in the Original Voices of the Authors too in electronic preservation devices. Maybe you're thinking along those lines. She said. It makes for very interesting reading. This may just be the start of that process. So please go on. I am sure to have a great time listening to you.

I don't know about you or anyone else having a great time listening to my croaky voice, but let me go on to read what I've got here. What is an accident? An accident is something that happens – anything which happens which is not planned for to happen, and happens suddenly when the person or persons to whom it is happening or happens to, is going or are going in totally different ways, and usually have negative or undesireable consequences or results. Usually, yes, or more often than not, because to have an accident or any accident bringing about positive or desireable consequences or results is a rarity, to which extent, I do not know where this book falls into as a product of an accident, whether the result is positive or negative – desireable or undesireable – good or bad. That belongs to the Reader to say in the end. How did I get here? He asked, taking his eye away from the book open in front of him. How did we get here?

To the accident that this book is? You've gaat to tell me that. Pattie Dazzle said, speaking for the third time since she was offered the Chair to sit down where she sat with her gadgets on full display, plus her pen with which she scribbled, shaking her head as the man she had come to speak with on appointment after a very long time of making it, spoke on and on.

I'm gonna tell you. He said without looking at her. But I'm naat telling just you. Whatever I tell you is the same thing that anyone and everyone who gets a chance to lay their hands on a copy of this book will be told as they read. I am not going off the text of the script before me.

That's just fine. Pattie Dazzle said as she wrote something down on the page open before her. Can I have coffee, please? Or is that too much to ask? Your Office is freezing cold. She asked and gave her reason as to why she asked for what she had asked for.

He looked at her with great surprise and then put his right hand on his chin.

Yes, yes, yes, Coffee, yes! Professor Olanrewaju suddenly said, as though he had just heard what she had told him. Only that while the Coffee may be fire hot as you drink it, it makes the fire burning inside of me dead cold.

Fire inside of you dead cold? She asked him in horror.

Yes. He said. My fire will be dead cold the moment we break off for Coffee! But can I help it? Can I help it? You are freezing cold. And I'm supposed to be a Black man used to the fire of the scorching Sun than the cold of the Mountain top. Isn't that strange? Very strange?

I'm sorry, Professor Abejaiday. But I must have a hot cup of Coffee now or else I'll be in trouble.

O my Goodness! He screamed as he stood up.

Pattie Dazzle stood up too. She walked right into his chest and got lost in him in a fire hot embrace.

Professor Abejide Olanrewaju did not see that coming. Pattie Dazzle planted a red rose flower on the fertile soil of his space which she had effectively covered, feeling good, better and better than good and better and better as she covered more of the soil that she had opened in which to sow for the future.

When they broke loose and free, Professor Abejide Olanrewaju hissed in pain as he said You know, Pattie, that I talked about accidents not long ago, don't you? And as I said about every known accident in the world, I did not see this accident coming. But please tell me. Tell me the way you were when you acted as the mouth piece of your fold when you gave me your hint about the Nobel. Did you also see this coming yourself? He asked her. Did you see it coming?

My dear Prof. Pattie Dazzle called him. I don't think we are in the best of settings here for me to answer this question. This place is inappropriate for that, and I'm still freezing cold, and still need my cup of steaming Coffee desperately!

The two people stood facing each other within a very reasonable distance from each other. Nobody quite knew what next to do. They just stared at each other for different reasons under the organ under their left chests.

After a very long silence, Pattie Dazzle spoke again.

I've fixed a fairly comfortable Apartment for myself somewhere down town to stay at the end of my business with you. Shall I request that we take that business down there to continue what else we need to do?

Professor Abejide Olanrewaju did not answer. He mopped at her.

Okaii. She said. This is the Address. I'll take a Cab. You drive after me after I've gone out of sight of this place. I'll be waiting for you. One more thing. We will come back here in different cars too. When we're back, you'll please place a call to your wife and ask her to please meet us here to be a part of what she feared that I told her will never be. She must meet us back here and see us do what for I came from the City of Angels to do here! Maybe I dazzle, afterall?

Pattie Dazzle stormed out of the Professor's Office. And moments, thereafter, she was gone. Gone into thin air, leaving the owner of the Office gasping for breath and completely lost in his own thoughts.

This was how my first babies came. Professor Abejide Olanrewaju told Pattie Dazzle one hour or so after he had been with her in the very posh Apartment which she had herself described as very modest, moments ago in his Office. Life follows the same pattern in every circumstance that I know, no matter in what Culture, Geography or Humanity. You know that something is about to happen from the word go, and yet you do not know that it is happening or that it is going to happen or what it is really. It happens anyway, and it is given a ready-made name – accident. Is there ever an accident anywhere in the world, for instance, this one? I don't think so. I don't. I don't because everyone saw it coming even before it took it's roots to begin to form.

Abejaiday. Pattie Dazzle called him softly. This is as much an accident as it is not. And, therefore, it fits perfectly into the pattern of every accident. What is that pattern? We also know and say that every accident is caused. Or don't we? That is the truth. I had nothing of what we both have been through here during the better part of the last one hour or so on my mind at all, the day that I had to address you on behalf of my Colleagues. Your wife caused it after she said what she said and I responded the way that I did. That was it. I told myself that this accident was gonna happen! And I didn't have to do anything extraordinary for that to happen. And today, I feel great that here we are making it happen. Yes. People should learn to keep their distance from where they ain't directly involved or called in to act what we know they are and can act. So when you are ready, we will go back to your Office to continue our agreed discourse. And as I said earlier, you must invite your wife for her to come and see us and to draw her own Conclusions that we mean no harm to her. Or if she has other eyes for her to see what we know that is there for to see.

Life has a wicked way of replicating whatever has happened before as time moves in it's unchangeable and unstoppable motion to the future as the fires of it's sons and daughters of the past die in order that it will continue to move in it's known and sure trajectory. Professor Abejide Olanrewaju told himself as he remained stone cold silent.

I wonder who is older between the two of us. Pattie said, not as a question but as an observation which she had suddenly decided to make.

When he still remained silent, she spoke on. She was on a Course that was irreversible.

I have a feeling that you are slightly older than me, great. If I am older, too bad, but that won't make the Guinness Book of Records, anyway. It will be great all the same for Pattie who I dazzle.

He understood where she was coming from. And he respected her for it. She had no business where she was. He told himself. Pattie Dazzle should be teaching in the University. Yes. With her Masters Degrees in two distinct Fields of Study and an M. Phil in a related Third – Economics, Sociology, Political Science. What was she doing with all those Degrees in someone else's Media Empire? He wondered. Maybe she is where she ought to be. He thought to himself. Maybe. You need a very high level of Information in the Information Highway of today's World to be relevant in any Media outfit. The competition is break neck. He thought. And only the tough survive and make a mark for everyone else to see.

And then his mind veered to the Media Greats of the World that everyone knew. He went through their names, ending with Pattie Dazzle.

I guess I'll have to go ahead of you just as you gat here ahead of me, since it is to my place that we are heading now. He said as he rose from the posh bed that had seen some turmoil in the recent past that had turned cold as the ice that endured now. Yes, hot and cold rule the world. He told himself.

She got lost once more in the shade of his powerful chest and watered the roses that she had planted way back in his Office and in here moments ago, and then disengaged from him when she was done fertilizing them.

He did not do anything. Neither did he say anything. He just stared into space.

I'll catch up with you. Pattie Dazzle said, looking at him with an air of arrogance and satisfaction. But please place your wife on notice that she should meet us there doing what I've come to do with you. Everyone kept to the terms of the agreement that they had reached very freely without anyone of them having to invoke any Amendment of any Constitution to do or not to do anything.

After watching them go through the rigours of reading, note taking and silences in between for well over an hour, Mrs. Abimbola Olanrewaju begged her husband and the Top Radio and Television Host Fire-Cracker of the Journalist that Pattie Dazzle was known to be, to plead with them to please break for a moment for the late lunch which she had brought along with her for the three of them to eat.

That shouldn't take too long. She said.

The two people did as she prayed them to do – break from what they were doing. But when Pattie Dazzle saw the typical Will Rock food which Abimbola displayed on the massive Conference Table, she was very happy to offer her kind apologies to be excluded from the eating.

Pattie Dazzle gave two reasons why she would not eat. Two related and unrelated reasons.

One was the reason which was very obvious for everyone to see. The food was strange to her. Very strange to her. Her stomach was not built for to accommodate them.

Reason number two stunned Lady Abimbola.

I've come here after many weeks of Appointments, Disappointments, Re-scheduling, Cancelations and more Appointments, to do my legitimate job as a Journalist. And I intend to keep my focus there in doing just that job. With the stories that we read and hear now and again coming from your part of the World, it is also very easy for a Cup of Tea or Coffee to cause disaster or for it to go by another name – Gratification or Bribe. To partake of this elaborate Luncheon that you have brought here, cannot be anything devoid of one of those things – Disaster and Gratification or Bribe, Madam. Let me, therefore, provide you the space and time that you must require for you to enjoy your meal while I run down town to also have a bite and come back. She said. Maybe one hour. Or not much longer than that.

And come back? Abimbola asked her, wide eyed.

I thought so, Madam! Pattie Dazzle said. But how do you mean? We break off for the day?

Abimbola looked at her husband for him to have a say or his way on that question which she was very sure that he heard very well too.

Well. He said. I had thought that we could finish what we were doing today. But from what you have suggested, it makes sense for us to have a break here, especially as Pattie Dazzle isn't eating with us but is going to search for what to eat in town. There's always another opportunity for us to meet and continue with what we have been doing and have done all day.

Pretty good. Pattie Dazzle said. I have to call my Office to ask for one more day then. You call me when you are ready for me tomorrow. Have a wonderful night, Madam. She said. You too, Prof. She added.

Pattie. Mrs. Abimbola called Pattie Dazzle, smiling wryly. I thought we've gotten over Jide being ready for you? Aren't we?

She did not allow Pattie Dazzle to say anything. She had made her feelings known.

That's okay. She said. And that was how that conversation ended.

Professor Abejide Olanrewaju made another stop at Pattie Dazzle's posh Apartment. This time he got there one hour before he told his wife that he was coming back home to her for the day.

I've got only one hour to be with you. He told her.

That's a lot of time in the circumstance. You're very smart. Pattie told her very welcome Guest. But before you say or do anything, please assure me that our tomorrow is also beginning from here with Breakfast for two. Do you promise? Can I trust you?

I ain't gaat no problem with that. Professor Abejide Olanrewaju said as he got lost in the labyrinth that he had come to willingly, after all the dilly-dallying of the past that his Office saw him act, by in some cases doing nothing, but only consenting.

# CHAPTER TWENTY

# VOID DISAPPEARING AND APPEARING

When you are dealing with any person who you think or know that knows as much about life as you yourself know or may know – who you may know may even know more than you know, you have to be very careful. And that is my take on what a wife and a husband are. They must know nearly everything in equal measure, only tilting to one side or the other side as a matter of depth – depth only and in particular subject areas only. The outline is the same. I am happy, Pattie, that you are listening to me without interrupting me. I am very happy that that is what you are doing. Afterall, what you came to Baltimore to do is to listen to this man called Professor blah-blah-blah for you to do what you want to do with it after you have listened to him and are gone back where you came from. I am happy to be here. And I am here by choice, not only because you asked me to come for whatever we should be having in front of us – Breakfast or a Fast Break? It doesn't matter. I have taken certain decisions where I am coming from in order to make sure that we cover our tracks very well. My wife will be back to my office very shortly. This time she is coming with our two children. I was supposed to deliver the Speech from which this book we are reading out aloud was derived, to an Audience that included all of them, afterall. So they will all be there while Pattie and I dazzle them doing only legitimate official business. So what have you got for the Breakfast that you promised me? He suddenly stopped musing to ask Pattie Dazzle sporting a see through morning dress that had all the traits of a killer tigress about to strike about it.

I'm here. She said softly. Here totally for you as you would want to feel me, sound me and crush me from what is left of me after the last time that you did that which I cannot remember now but still feel all over me.

No wonder Dazzle is her last name. Professor Olanrewaju thought as he surveyed her Engineering Design. Dazzle should have been her first name. He thought. Yes. He said. Yes. He continued to say until he could not say anything else, neither know where he was exactly, nor how he was going to end doing what he was doing or when that end anyone where and how he was would envisage was going to be.

She was awake and quite alive to her own part of the bargain, and did not disappoint him or let herself down.

I am Pattie. She told herself to reassure herself. I party only with who I want or desire to party with. This man here meets all my parry standards. So I just don't care. I don't care! She screamed inside of her even as she heard his sigh of release and relief signal to her that touch down had happened.

In another twenty minutes or so Professor Abejide Olanrewaju was poring over a pile of papers at his Professorial Desk.

His wife Mrs. Abimbola Olanrewaju and their two Children arrived first. Abimbola was surprised that the woman responsible for their presence there at that point in time was not there yet. What must have gone wrong? She wondered aloud?

She phoned in. Abejide told his wife. To say that she had to make several phone calls to reschedule many other Interview Appointments that she had secured before to keep, and for her to file her Maiden Report on what she has gathered already with her interface with me here and there.

I see. Abimbola said. So she is going to do a piece meal Report? She asked.

Not after that her First Report. He told his anxious wife. She has to let her Employers know that she is not playing or doing nothing here. You know America. Apart from their standards being very high, they don't give room to anyone for them to fool around. They justify every dime that they spend on any Project, no matter what that Project is. He said. That's what they are.

I know. Abimbola said. That is why they make the kind of progress that they make on all Frontiers and facets of life. Nothing is too small or too insignificant or too big for them to take on with the same zeal, with the same dedication and hunger to satisfy or to feed. She agreed with him.

You got it right. Professor Abejide said, a flash of Brighton and Baltimore passing through his mind's eye.

Before anyone of them could say anything else, Pattie Dazzle breezed in, panting for breath.

Ah! Pattie! You are breathless, why? Professor Olanrewaju asked her not sure if his why was for her panting for breath or why she had come in later than his wife.

I'm sorry. She said. I had to walk upstairs instead of take the elevator. I was avoiding running into someone in the same Trade with me. I have to keep our secrets secret, you know? Yes, I had to.

That's okay. Professor Olanrewaju said. So do you want to catch your breath for a few minutes? Bimbo Junior and Jide Junior will be Members of our Audience with the Senior Bola here. He said, pointing at the three people that made up his Quartet.

Good to see you again. Professor Olanrewaju's wife, Abimbola told Pattie Dazzle, deliberatly avoiding calling her by her name, hating both names Pattie that sounded to her like someone who was adept at parting a River as with a magic wand, and Dazzle even more obvious, and so more frightful than Pattie.

Thank you, Madam. Pattie Dazzle said. And how are you little ones? She asked the twins, smiling at them.

What do you say? Abimbola asked them.

We are fine, Auntie! They sang as they would sing a Nursery Rhyme.

I think I'm ready to go. Pattie Dazzle said, placing her equipment where she placed them on the previous day, and her wide note book in front of her, the page on which she wrote last staring at her like a silent witness to many other notes that had been written where else it did not know by any name. Crime notes or Diary, maybe.

The Void that I showed on Slide One progressively moved from one stage of development of the image that we saw there to assume other dimensions. He started to read, sounding very business-like. There was the man representing nature who transformed from a Military sensibility to something between and betwixt Military and Civilian and looked like a man in penury at first, and then became a man of immense Power and Wealth once again, and even in greater measure than at the time when he led with Guns and Tanks at his Command.

None of the examples that I have here are about my country Will Rock. No. None. They are about countries on the African Continent called The Dark Continent by those who discovered the New World Order after the Old Order had taken their firm roots. But no country in that Third World taxonomy is free from all the plunderings and misrule that the country of the man in constant transformation is from. Will Rock may be guilty of the same thing too, who knows? Who knows? I don't myself.

What is the root cause of this malaise? What is the root cause of the misrule, plundering and the brazen institutionalization of Corruption and the dearth of Accountability? The people of those countries are to blame for their docility. They are squarely to blame for their tolerance of the intolerable that seems to have no limit. But they are not solely to blame. The Leaders of the so called First World and Second World are to blame too. They are to blame for their Double Standards. They are to blame for their standards which allow the Leaders of the Impoverished Third World countries to feel emboldened and patronized to carry out their plundering and misrule.

Professor Abejide Olanrewaju suddenly got up from where he sat reading from his book. He pushed the huge book away from him.

He started pacing the large space that his Office had up and down, gesturing as he spoke as though he had been seized by the spirit of hysteria or something far worse than that. An Alarm Bell flashed past his wife's mind, making her stare vacantly into space and beginning to tremble as though she would collapse under her weight.

Whose soul is my book asking to stir? Whose soul? Which Nation? Is it Russia? It is England? Is it Germany or France? Or any of their Allies or Enemies real as well as perceived wrongly, rightly or imagined? I have it in my book! It is here, even though it may not be in the order or the sequence that I am speaking about them now that I have dropped the book. But come to think of it, is what we are considering limited to countries and their Leaders? What about the people that they are leading or are supposed to lead? And the people who are just there, whether they are being led or let down? How much of trust do we have in each other as Members of the same Humanity? What, for instance, was the tenor of the first words that you spoke to yourselves, my dear wife Bimbo and Ombudswoman Pattie Dazzle? Was it not one of mistrust, distrust and total lack of faith one in the other? What about now? Has that picture changed? Why do we derive pleasure in raking up problems from where there is none and from where there should be none? Why are we the way that we are?

Jide! Abimbola called out loud for her husband as he rattled on. Jide! She called him again.

Still he did not answer. Neither did he behave in any manner to suggest that he heard what she said or that he knew that she was there in his space in the first place. Nor did he cut the picture of a man who had the faintest idea that there was any one else where he was, let alone the fact that his twins were there or that a Top Journalist, whatever her name was, was also there.

Pattie. Abimbola called out loudly for Pattie Dazzle. Please do something. Help me to do something. Let us stop him. Let us stop him. I have heard about *too* much learning making someone mad before. I don't want that to happen to my husband. Please help me! Jide! My dear husband, Jide! She called out, the twins looking with amazement and complete loss at their father in his esoteric ways. They also looked at their mother in her state of stupefaction but did nothing else.

Professor Abejaidaay! Pattie Dazzle called him, looking completely stunned and shattered. Professor Abejaidaay! Pattie Dazzle called out for him again, shaking her head from left to right to catch his attention which was not happening. He did not bother about anyone in that his space.

Suddenly he stopped talking and stood at a spot as though he heard what he heard from very distant lands, and waited to make sure about what he thought he had heard.

# CHAPTER TWENTY-ONE

# JOURNALISTS ARE ALWAYS PREGNANT

Professor Abejaidaay! Pattie Dazzle called out for him one more time.

My dear Jide! Abimbola called him, also very loudly, looking all the more alarmed.

Professor Abejide Olanrewaju looked vacantly in his wife's eyes as though she were a complete stranger – a stranger he was yet to meet.

What am I talking about? What am I not talking about? He started again to speak but this time more to himself than to anyone else.

I am talking about everything! I am talking about everything! Yes! That is what I am doing. And yet do not be fooled. Do not be deceived! I am not talking about anything. I am talking about something and yet I am not talking about anything. What do you think that I am doing? Just talking? Maybe. Maybe I am just talking! Yes. You be the judge from what you hear me speak about. Or from what you think that I am talking about.

Mrs. Abimbola Olanrewaju walked up to Professor Abejide Olanrewaju and hugged him.

Come and sit down. She told him, leading him to the Conference Table beside which there were posh sofas. She led him to sit gently in the three sitter there, she herself beginning to shiver feverishly.

I think you should leave him alone for now. Abimbola told Pattie Dazzle who was totally confused.

Maybe I am to blame. O, maybe. Maybe I am to blame for all these. And I feel so guilty, O! O! O! Pattie Dazzle said, feeling very sorry for what she was experiencing in broad daylight.

You say that you are to blame for this? How do you mean, Pattie? And you feel sorry? I don't understand. How do you mean, Pattie, that maybe you are responsible for this my husband's condition? Please tell me so that I can understand even if not perfectly. Mrs. Abimbola Olanrewaju said.

There you go again, Madam, with perfectly! Perfectly. Pattie Dazzle said. Is there any perfection in our world? I don't know. Can't you sense it yourself – that I just might be responsible for what you are saying is the truth about his condition? Would this have been if not for Pattie Dazzle? Would this happen if I were not here to make him talk about his book, to make him read to me – to read his book with him?

O that, Pattie. I get that. I understand that. But I have to thank you for that too. Honestly, I have to thank you for that. Mrs. Abimbola Olanrewaju said, looking at Pattie Dazzle in a very strange way.

What do I do, Madam? Pattie Dazzle asked Mrs. Abimbola Olanrewaju.

That's a very good question. A very good question to ask at this point. She said. What do you think? Mrs. Abimbola Olanrewaju threw the question back at Pattie Dazzle.

Maybe I should go. Maybe I should go. But I have not finished my job. Pattie Dazzle said musingly, betraying certain emotions that even she herself could not imagine were on display on her face.

That's okay, my sister. Abimbola said. But at this point, don't you think that it is more important for you to consider his well being than what you came to do with him? She asked her.

To do with him, Madam? Pattie Dazzle asked in fury. I came to talk with him about his book only! Only about his book! She said angrily.

I know. I know, Pattie. Mrs. Abimbola said. Please sit down for a moment and let us put our heads together as friends, as colleagues – as what else? I wonder. As what else? Maybe as Members of the same Humanity – the Humanity that he was talking about not long ago.

That's interesting. Pattie Dazzle said as she sat down next to Mrs. Abimbola Olanrewaju. Good to hear from you. Good to know that you believe that we are all Members of the same Humanity. I can also read people's minds, Madam. I know what you have on your mind right now! Do you want to bet with me? Whether I am going to Portray him in any bad light on account of the accident that has happened. Is that not what you are thinking about now? I know that very well as the reason you have suddenly begun to talk to me patronizingly. And I very much understand. I perfectly understand. And let me assure you that I will breathe no word of what we both have seen here during the past many moments. It happens. I have seen it happen many times before. He will be okaiiyy. He is fine. But as you suggested, I will cork my pen from here and leave. I have enough materials from him already for my scoop which I am grateful to him that he has given to me already. I shall speak with him on the phone to fill any blank spaces that I find needs filling. Let me thank you also for your fantastic handling of his tip over. He needs you more than he needs me or anyone else right now. You are married to a great man whose greatness will continue to grow.

Thank you, my sister. Mrs. Abimbola Olanrewaju said. I am happy that you understand.

Perfectly! Perfectly, Madam. Pattie Dazzle said. Let me go. Let me go, Madam.

I am afraid of you, Pattie, if you say that you have to go now. Mrs. Abimbola Olanrewaju said. Yes. Very much.

You are afraid of me, Madam? Why? Pattie Dazzle asked her in fear.

Yes, I mean that I am afraid of you – not only you but every Journalist. You people are all the same. You are pregnant. And heartless when you want to be.

How do you mean I am pregnant? And heartless? Pattie Dazzle asked her.

I mean, Pattie, that you are pregnant. Don't misunderstand me. You Journalists are always pregnant – yes, pregnant with ideas – pregnant with the seeds being sown inside of you and to take roots – to fester inside of you which, when you decide to bring out, is dangerous most of the time – very dangerous and devastating to those who you target. That is what I mean. You are dangerous – people like you, in particular, because you have everything going for you. Who will refuse to give you an appointment to speak to you? What man is there in the world who will shun the chance to do anything that you ask him to do with you? You dazzle. Yes, you dazzle. Which is strangely your father's name and not your first name. You are pretty and dazzle. Maybe his mother dazzled his father!

Ha! Madam! Are you saying that you have to thank me for your husband –I mean our Author's condition? And then turn round to hate me? Pattie Dazzle asked her.

I don't know about our Author, Pattie. But yes, I have to thank you for my husband's condition as we both have seen it. Just think for a moment what this could mean, if it had not been for you – that this happened in a very public place like the Auditorium or like the McDonald's at which we made our first acquaintance? Wouldn't that have been outrageous? For it to happen before the whole wide world? That is my take – that is where I am coming from. Because it is you – only you talking with him – only to you that he was reading! If you agree with me, we can keep it out of the attention, the knowledge and understanding of the world for now. God! I hope he recovers! Yes, and that what you said is true – that he will get over it – because everyone like him suffers it once in a while – maybe once in a constant while. And so if he gets over it, thanks to you, no one will get to know. Ever! That's why I say I've got you to thank for it. Mrs. Abimbola Olanrewaju said.

Madam! I have always had this feeling since my first encounter with you that you are in every way like your husband our Writer and Speaker! You know what I mean? Yes, you are, like him, so lucid, so so philosophical in your pronouncements, that I have developed a world of respect for you. I tell you what? I must assure you now, if I wasn't going to do that before – I mean now, you must believe me that I will never breathe a word of what we both have seen and experienced here in Baltimore – yes – what started here in this his Office and shifted base. I assure you. Pattie Dazzle said.

Thank you, Pattie, for your promise, even though I must own that sometimes I cannot understand the entire extent of what you say – like when you talk about what we both saw and experienced, starting in Baltimore and in this his Office. And shifting base? But here again, I must assure you that I perfectly understand why you are saying what you are saying, as well as the circumstances leading up to it. Mrs. Abimbola Olanrewaju said.

Madam, you mean that you understand even that? The circumstances leading up to it? I am amazed and will be forever shocked if that also happens to be true! I must say then that the two of you are the same in nearly every way! Pattie Dazzle said, looking away from Mrs. Abimbola Olanrewaju.

O thank you, if that is supposed to be a compliment. But you know that nobody would like to go through what he has just gone through? I wouldn't want to share that trait with him, good as all the other traits are, you know? Mrs. Abimbola Olanrewaju said, looking all the more worried.

Yes Madam. That I perfectly understand! And you must believe me that I do!

# CHAPTER TWENTY-TWO

# EPILOGUE

# THREE POEMS, MADAM, THREE POEMS

Five days after Pattie Dazzle went back to the City of Angels, she looked over what she put down in her Diary as thoughts that ran through her mind as she looked out the window of Southern's Big Bird Flying her back where she had come from.

She turned on her Lap Top and struck away.

After she was done, she called the Mail Man attached to her Office.

See. She told him. This must get to it's destination today. It is still AM. So you must tell the Carriers that the Addressee has to read what's in there today! I mean today! Today or else I'll sue for Default and for Damages for Non Performance. You gaat that? She asked The Mail Man who blinked, I gaat you Ma'aam.

In twenty five or so minutes he was back at her door hailing Madam, your Mail is gone! Expect a phone call before our Sunset today. He said very confidently.

That is great. Pattie said, smiling. She flung a bill at him.

The Mail Man smiled as he took the Dollar bill from her, not doing anything to make sure whose silhouette was on the bill – whether it be Thomas Jefferson, Abraham Lincoln or John Fitzgerald Kennedy.

Always a pleasure to serve you, Ma'am. He said as he saluted, his cap steady on his head.

I know. She said, smiling again. That you always deliver. Pretty good!

This came via my Office early this afternoon. Professor Abejide Olanrewaju told Abimbola his wife as he pointed the Parcel at her when he arrived back home that evening – it was early evening, the Sun setting but still glowing as it travelled West home to sleep.

Really? She asked him surprised. Who knows I'm here to write from –let me see – looks like, ah!

It's from Los Angeles. Professor Abejide Olanrewaju said as he sat down, looking very moody and exhausted.

Is that so? She asked, looking all the more surprised.

Who could be writing to her from the City of Angels? Who did she know there? She wondered.

Abimbola led her husband to his Dinner Table, and once he began to eat, tore the Parcel which she had carried in her hand all along open and went through what it held hidden inside it.

It's from Pattie! She screamed inside her, placing her left hand over her really big stomach.

It's from Pattie Dazzle. She told herself as she read –

My dear Madam. I try my hands on many things as you can see, while my heart and mind direct me wherever they wander.

Poetry is one of them – one of my hobby horses. But what have I written about here?

What have I written?

Sometimes we don't know what we write or mean. That's the way it is sometimes. Sometimes, yes. Still we write, anyway.

You know we agreed to get in touch the day I left, assuring you that everything will be fine. Didn't I? I'm sure you remembered that I did.

I'm sure no one has had to disprove me? I will like to think so. Or am I wrong?

Share my love to all you will, especially to the two who are two and are from two but are one. Pattie. She signed off.

And then Mrs. Abimbola Olanrewaju began to read the main course that she had been served.

## MAYBE I DON'T KNOW

Why was I telling you
What I had to tell you,
Not just yesterday
But everyday
That dawns
After business is done?
Why was I placing
The calls to you, tracing
The paths I have gone
No matter how far gone?
I don't know why
Nor do I have reasons why
I had to do
What I had to do.
Maybe something is wrong?
Wrong with me all along?
That maybe is why.
Yes, that may just be why.
Now that I know,
Let me see how I go
From now in doing
Anything worth doing
As I go my way
From day to day
If you still have a hold
On everything in my fold.
Rethink your course

And nothing do without cause.

Enough is enough.
Yes, I have had enough.

**WHERE, YOUR GUITAR?**

So where,
Where's your Guitar?
And your Sister
Who's better
Than you to strum
For harmony to drum
Sweet in my ears
And of every hearers'?

Professor Abejide Olanrewaju's wife Mrs. Abimbola Olanrewaju closed the pages containing the Poems that she had just read, completely lost in thought on what to make of them. She cast occasional glances at her husband as he ate in silence, and closed her eyes, trying very hard to figure out what the pen pusher from the City of Angels meant to convey to her through the medium of those lovely Teasers of Poetry and the introductory lines preceding the words in elevated flight mode.

Soon she was snoring. Professor Abejide Olanrewaju could hear the hissing sounds of her snoring as he lifted one piece of meat or food into his mouth. The pregnancy had taken a huge toll on her. He thought, feeling sorry for what he had done to her to bring her where she was, not having any idea what lay on her mind as she slept or what the papers on her laps contained inside of them.

Fffffffffffffuuuuuuuuuuuuuffffffffffffffffffuuuuuuuuuuuuuuu she snored peacefully, tempering the storm raging in her mind that she had carried to the world no one knew.

The End

# ABOUT THE AUTHOR

Dumo Kaizer Johnny Oruobu was born in Ogurama in Degema District of Nigeria's Rivers State of The Niger Delta Region to Christie and Chief Kaizer John Oruobu on September 22 in 1952. He studied at Baptist Day School, Old Bakana, Zixton Grammar School, Ozubulu, Government Comprehensive Secondary School, Borikiri, County Grammar School, Ikwerre-Etche and Baptist High School, Port Harcourt between 1966 and 1973; and in 1975 went on to study English Language and Literature at Nigeria's prestige premier University of Ibadan, graduating in November, 1978. He is an accomplished Singer, Poet, Inspirational Speaker and Preacher of The Word of God. He is a Prize Writer in all the genres, an accomplished Print, Radio and Television Journalist and is firmly rooted in Entertainment, Advertising, Marketing and Public Relations. He has written well over eighty Novels out of which eight have been published, all in 2016. He is a Fellow of Nigeria's Institute of Corporate Administration and is a Member of The Nigerian Institute of Public Relations. He holds two Traditional Chieftaincy Titles – Anyawo XI of Ogurama and Amaibi Dokibo So Bomabo, Se Erena XII of Kalabari. He loves travels and people, and makes friends very easily.

Printed in the United States
By Bookmasters